Praise for Lost and Found

"Mona Soliman writes with unflinching honesty and clear-eyed compassion...Her characters are as real as mirrors and sentiment never crosses the line to sentimentality."

— Jessica Tilles, author of *Loving Simone*

"An inspiring tale of a woman's journey to find peace in the choices she's made. Lost and Found is further confirmation that there is a rainbow after the storm."

—V Helena author of *His Love is Complete: A Compilation of Poems, Short Stories and Other Libations of the Heart*

"Mona Soliman's "Lost and Found" is a heartwarming, thought provoking masterpiece. It is a revealing, soul-searching journey into the depths of a woman's love for her child. Ms. Soliman's style is uniquely engrossing, passionate, enlightening, sensitive and funny. Her story is a must read for all women who have been derailed from their path and also for those who have been fortunate to find their way. There is something for everyone. She teaches that through faith and a belief in a power greater than ourselves, all things are possible. Kudos to Mona for a job well done. I can't wait for the next one!"

— Errol J. Bailey, MD, author of *Mr. Dream Merchant*, screenwriter and executive producer of *The Last Adam*

Cathie —
May all your
journeys be
as lovely as you!

Lost
AND **FOUND**

Best —
Mona
S.

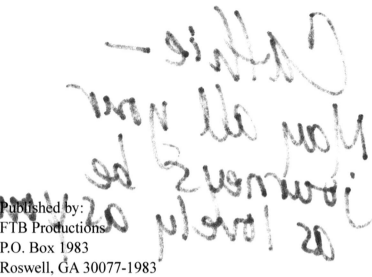

Published by:
FTB Productions
P.O. Box 1983
Roswell, GA 30077-1983
www.singlemomfaithnation.com

ISBN: 978-0-9890077-0-2

Library of Congress Control Number: 2013933222

Disclaimer:
This is a work of fiction. Names, characters, businesses, places, events and incidents are either the products of the author's imagination or used in a fictitious manner. Any resemblance to actual persons, living or dead, or actual events are purely coincidental.

Lost and FOUND

Mona Soliman

To my rainbow star,
Keep shining, keep reaching and be all you were created to be.

To Trevor,
I know you are out there.

ACKNOWLEDGMENTS

First and foremost my humbled thanks to the Infinite Spirit that resides inside of me and all your many angels that keep urging me to ask, seek and knock on my journey of life. Thank you for faith and grace.

To my mother and father who created me and additionally with my step mother for their never ending support to live every dream I ever attempted, even when my choices made no sense. Thank you for loving me.

To my rainbow star who gives me light every day to be better and guides my way when I have lost mine. He is both the reason I started this book and finished it. Thank you for your unconditional love that is the light of my life.

To my attorney, Tanya Mitchell Graham, who through this process was truly my attorney AND counselor. You are gifted beyond your education. Thank you for your poise when I assuredly lost mine. Thank you for teaching me to see the big picture and for serving your people when justice comes undone.

To my very talented editor and book cover designer, Jessica Tilles of TWA Solutions, for your tireless direction and wise advise to bring this project to reality. It almost didn't happen! Thank you for putting up with my numerous questions and revisions along the way at all hours of the night. Thank you for you.

To my many friends, Steve K, Ritston B, Eric C, Valerie H, Erroll B, Rod E, Kim S, Sharee M, Michael S, Angela & Alan G, Krysta H., Isaac R, Marguerite B, Marva L, Michelle B, Heather C, Nicole S, Nicole L, Leslie K, Renica S, Michael M, Ken S, Wayne V, Jerry D and others known and even those unknown (forgive me if I forgot to mention any because there have been so many), thank you for your endless support, encouragement and prayers that gave me strength and courage that I can't begin to express. I am humbled to call you my friend and to have crossed your path and to know you. We are truly a force greater in numbers than in ourselves. Thank you for your presence in my life!

To all who may read this story. May it fill you with love and light to have faith, trust and to believe in all you were created to be. Be true to yourself. Thank you for sharing.

Note:

Thank you to Google who is my BFF—for the countless sources available and research information I was able to obtain regarding so much in this process and along the journey.

One
CHOICES

I COULDN'T REMEMBER THE LAST time I'd been kissed that way. Maybe I never had been. Or, maybe if you want something badly enough, you make yourself feel things that aren't really there.

It was a perfect evening under the moonlit sky and the temperature was balmy enough to make dinner on the patio comfortable. However, I was anxious to leave the restaurant, as I glanced around, people watching, thinking I'd rather be at home curled up with a good book. I wasn't attracted to Clyde and thought his conversation was drier than sand, recalling the same impression I had upon our first meeting when I was on vacation a month ago, even though I agreed to dinner after his repeated and persistent invitations. The crowd was down to merely a few in the later evening. Although the night was still young, the day had been a long one—six hours later—and after a few of Clyde's unwelcomed hints and my continual declinations to join him at his hotel to spend the night, I wanted to go home and take a bath. He didn't push, but as I turned my head to thank him for dinner and announce my interest to call it a night, that's when Clyde leaned in, caressed my face and kissed me tenderly on the lips. The kiss was deliberate, slow and warm. I hesitated, as everything seemed to move in slow motion, before realizing I was in a daze. The clear evening sky and bright full moon romantically lighting up the night, the breeze blowing up my sundress, cooling my body under the humid air, and even the bold red wine Sangria I was drinking didn't tempt me anymore to want to join him at his hotel.

Over the next few weeks of conversations, Clyde invited me to come see him for a weekend in Chicago. Although I was torn inside to what I felt—out of my boredom and curiosity—I accepted, rationalizing that maybe relationships happen this way; where one person pursues the other with persistence to win the heart of the other person and they acquiesce over time to the admiration and charm of their suitor. What did I know about relationships, after all, except how to pick the wrong ones? Maybe if I gave Clyde a chance and got to know him more, I could find something redeeming and we could evolve from there.

Clyde wasn't the usual type of man I was attracted to, as I preferred tall men with an athletic build, clean-shaven or neatly cut facial hair long enough to show off their facial bone structure. And, I was really attracted to a man with a confident walk and a wit that could keep up with my own.

Truthfully, I knew the chance of a relationship working with him was a long shot. Much like rationalizing every other aspect of my life, I created a statistical equation in my mind about dating. Complete with significance and variance, I realized that much like the advanced math we learn in school, it doesn't apply in the real world and we make dating and relationships harder than necessary. I avoided dating the good guys and almost sought the bad ones in some attempt to disprove a theory or dispel a myth, like convincing myself that a square is actually a circle with straight edges. Clyde wasn't particularly exciting, but he did have a medical degree from University of Pennsylvania, an accomplishment that drew me in to his good guy charm.

I considered possible scenarios to entertain his advances, deciding in the least I could simply try to see if there was more that I overlooked until I was ready to date seriously again. Over the coming weeks, I found myself justifying a long distance relationship with a built-in safety net and being able to control how fast it progresses.. That should have been the first sign, having an exit plan before having an entry.

Having recently gotten out a relationship I clearly wasn't ready for, I didn't want to be in another relationship. It seemed every relationship I'd been in was so one-sided and serious in such a short time, I looked for ways to make me the bad guy and exit without much confrontation. Maybe I'm not the relationship type. Or, maybe I am simply not good at it. I was forty and managed to run most suitors off or into the arms of other women since they were ready to marry. Maybe I was afraid of commitment. I divorced within six months of marrying a man I dated for six years because I didn't know what I wanted. My track record had spoken for itself.

It's easy to imagine a person being someone he is not. It's even easier to get caught up in a kiss when you have no idea what you want.

⟋

Over the next three months of occasional weekend visits between Charlotte and Chicago, I found nothing except shallowness and selfishness. With an overwhelming realization, I knew Clyde was not what I needed, although his edginess made me curious. In this case, my curiosity killed the cat and satisfaction didn't bring it back. The more I learned about him, the more I realized book sense had nothing to do with common sense, and his perspective on things was narcissistically skewed.

Within a few months, the travel became more monotonous than was fun, as my questions outnumbered my answers regarding who Clyde was. He was vague about everything, even down to what he ate for lunch. Our visits became fewer and farther between. Over the phone, we strained to find common interests to talk about beyond restaurant menus, the weather and sports scores. His apartment resembled a college dorm and when he visited me, I had an uneasy feeling about opening my personal space, preferring to blend in with tourist attractions, a movie or anything saving myself the façade of getting personal. I thought I was the one with problems, giving him the benefit of the doubt. That should have been my second sign.

After an understandably awkward first sexual experience, I hoped something would spark a fire from that single Casanova kiss to make me want to find out more about him. The spark didn't ignite any flames and I wasn't anxiously waiting until the next time I could see him on any sexual or other level to justify my involvement with him.

As fate would have it and life revealed itself; if you are so willing to ask the universe, I didn't have to.

After sprinting through the Los Angeles airport concourse to my gate, I made it on the plane in enough time that day to make my return flight to Charlotte. Randall was traveling on business there, deciding to take an earlier flight home to Chicago. Dropping my briefcase onto my seat to catch my breath, I noticed those same piercing eyes looking up from the magazine he was reading.

Though Clyde had said he was an old college buddy when we'd bumped into him at a restaurant last month, Randall had barely acknowledged him, staring at me intensely in a way that made me feel like he was photographing me, as if he knew he would see me again. It was a look of rage and pity between the two. I thought it nothing more than male egos colliding and past mistakes. That should have been my third sign.

My stomach gnawed at me immediately as I recognized Randall. I knew there was a purpose to this seemingly chance meeting.

After the usual pleasantries, I couldn't wait any longer. "How do you know Clyde?" I'd always known there was something off about Clyde that went deeper than my personal feelings about facial hair.

Randall spoke without pride and prejudice, with what almost sounded like forgiveness. Clyde had tried to take advantage of him on some real estate business deal he got involved in that went from bad to worse when Randall discovered his soon-to-be ex had been providing inside financial information to Clyde. In bed. And, from what I could figure, during the same time he was sleeping with me.

I didn't need any more signs. I wanted to be free.

Two
SERENITY

I SAT MOTIONLESS ON MY BATHROOM floor, hugging my knees close to my chest. The ceramic tile felt cold against my feet even as the morning sun beamed brightly through the oversized window. Tears streamed down my cheeks. Time was frozen as I sat there in a daze.

The alarm clock blared, forgetting I had set it last night for a Saturday morning run to distract me from what I didn't want to know. I woke up at five a.m. from a restless sleep needing to know. Now I did.

I lifted myself up from the floor to look at the four pregnancy tests neatly lined up on the basin countertop. Maybe I misread the tests. Maybe the different brands or different positive signs each meant something different. *The results did seem to appear way too fast to be accurate.* At forty, wasn't I entitled to have at least one irregular cycle in my lifetime? Between the business trips and the visits to see Clyde, all the travel certainly could have thrown it off. Maybe I had just been stressed. *I am strong.*

I rifled through the boxes in the garbage, searching for expiration stamps or percentages of inaccuracy—anything that could explain how this could happen, at this time, with this person. *I am strong,* I kept telling myself.

Weeks ago, I'd broken up with Clyde, swearing I would move on with my life after carelessly convincing myself to entertain a long distance relationship. I'd felt I owed him something because he tried hard to get me by adorning me with Tiffany trinkets and declaring me the 'last person he ever wanted to be with.' Admitting I'd made a mistake with him would be admitting, once again, that I really didn't know how to pick a decent man and I wasn't good at this relationship thing. All because of that one kiss.

I took a deep breath. *I am strong.* I sat on the bed and put on my running shoes.

My feet pounded the paved path along the Greenway, the abandoned railroad track that ran for miles in the industrial part of town, extending beyond state lines. When I first found the Greenway as a running trail, I soon became more inspired as I learned more of its history in the height of rail travel and freight transportation. It was still here. Once upon a time of a bustling industry, now gone, the Greenway had not fallen away.

Along my path, I ran a little faster over the wooded covered bridge with increased spirit, as I thought of each plank's strength and resilience bearing the weight of the cars that traveled this route. The same route that many cars travelled day after day and the planks repeatedly exposed to the severe elements of nature. They stood strong.

I felt as though I was flying as I ran; my body telling me how strong it was, my mind telling me I similarly could survive the harshest of elements and withstand the pressure and because something is gone doesn't mean something else can't change. It was something like a miracle. Even when you are weak, you are made stronger.

"I never thought I was going to have a child," I told my mother over the phone. "I thought I was getting old and my chances of having a child were already gone. But, God is showing me that life isn't about chances." I lay on the chaise, staring out the floor-to-ceiling windows at the Charlotte skyline. The sun was beginning to set.

"You'll be an amazing mom. Whenever you've put your mind to something, you've been exceptional, and if there would be a time you'd be ready, it would be now. You've built a life based on good choices." She hesitated. "Well, mostly good choices, but you've learned from the others."

Learning from your stubbornness in your teenage years was one thing. Learning to create a fantasy around a man you'd been flying to see in another city every few weekends, and allowing him to stay at your apartment when he visited you, when you really didn't know him and while he was sleeping with someone else, is another kind of education.

My computer chimed to let me know a new e-mail had arrived. I got up from the chaise to glance at it. *It is yet another message from Clyde begging my forgiveness.*

"Don't you think you should maybe try and give this guy a chance?" Mom asked a few minutes later. "Men need a little work and they sure don't always make sense."

"Mom, I appreciate what you are saying and I know there are reasons to stay with someone in this situation, like a child needs their father and maybe I didn't give the relationship enough time. I thought about all that. I've been thinking about it the last few days. But the thing is I ignored my intuition when I first met Clyde and I wanted to like him even though I didn't." I paused. "I think this time around it's important to be honest with myself. He's shown me who he his and I don't want to be with him."

"Do what is in your heart," Mom said compassionately. "I hear you and I'll support any decision you make. I am very proud of you and whatever you decide. You have nothing to be afraid of."

"You know, Mom, I don't feel afraid. I may have thought that if I ever had a child I'd be married or in love and sharing this with someone rather than doing it alone, but life isn't always straightforward that way." I thought about the Greenway that had been willed to happen by people who wanted it, believed in it and who built it, even after its time had come and gone. "Dreams may get deferred," I said. "Or diverted or even derailed. But, I know it's all with a purpose and I trust that everything will work out. Even when I made a poor decision or things happened and I didn't know how I'd survive, they always worked out. I have no reason to believe this will be any different, and having a baby is the most amazing thing. I'm going to be the best mom I can be. It's going to be hard not having family here, but I'll do my best." I walked over to the kitchen for something to eat. "God takes care of babies and fools, so I'm covered."

"Yes you are!" Mom laughed. "Olivia, one more thing. I hope you know and believe that God doesn't think you are less of a person for not being married. You are His creation and so is this baby. You have to trust that God uses people in others' lives for His glory. And, He is never wrong. This is serenity and accepting the things and people you can't change. Serenity is not about the fight; it's knowing when not to."

Clyde was one of them and our brief relationship was another.

I arrived to the office early that morning to prepare for my two o'clock client meeting. I was wearing my 'lucky' black Tahari skirt suit paired with an amethyst camisole and sling back black pumps. With my hair pulled back in a single, silky ponytail, it was all about confidence and comfort for the day and I was feeling it. Layla, my assistant, drew the vertical blinds in my office ever so slightly, the way she knew I liked, with the sun's natural light reflecting off the pale blue wall. She had made it in early and organized the work on my desk in order of priority with the important things highlighted on the left of my desk calendar—like appointments and deadlines and follow ups—and my things to do list to the right. The office décor was simple and contemporary with stainless steel and glass desks and meeting tables paired with deep-seated black cushioned couches and chairs.

I was Vice President of Media Marketing for an advertising firm. Layla and I were a two-woman team that worked with a mutual understanding that we would do whatever it took to get the job done, however long it took. I didn't require much outside of passion and integrity. Layla, a single mother of two, didn't require much outside of flexibility and healthcare for her family. We were a perfect fit.

I stared at her as she poked her head in the office, appreciating all she had to overcome. She was completely organized and meticulous, putting everything from her children's homework and play dates to board meetings and presentations into her data planner, all color-coded. Her children, ages six and nine, were positive, intelligent and well mannered. I could learn so much from her about being a single mother. She had recently divorced after her husband decided—to her what seemed literally overnight—that he didn't want to be married anymore and moved out of state. Two months prior to that, she lost her mother and best friend.

"I confirmed the appointment and we're set for two," Layla said. "Let me know when you're ready to send the presentation to the printer and I'll get the copies bound." She always got anxious before a presentation.

"You're the greatest!" I smiled, as she turned away. I meant that.

"Oh." She paused, turning back. "Can I leave early on Wednesday for Lila's recital? She got the lead," she pleaded, trying to sound nonchalant. *What pleadings would I have to make soon enough?* What if I couldn't make a presentation to investors because my water broke? Or, how would I tell a demanding client that I had to stay home to care for my infant that had some ailment that only a mom can make better?

"Yes, and videotape it. She's amazingly poised."

Layla was dressed in her always-fashionable best with her hair cut into a short shoulder length bob. "Wonder where she get's that?" Layla smiled.

Starting up the computer, I sipped my five-dollar decaf cinnamon java, calculating that it was a pleasure I'd have to cut way back on. Three javas a week, over forty weeks, could add up to months of diapers. I made a mental note to purchase a coffeemaker on my next superstore run and start brewing at home.

I had a string of new emails and just as I had thought, one was from Clyde. He had sent emails almost daily to say he screwed up, begging for my forgiveness in his usual self-serving way. Even though I wanted him out of my life forever, I knew I had to tell him about the baby, and soon. No matter what kind of person I thought he was, he had the right to know he had a child on the way. Although our relationship might have been built on my wishful thinking, that didn't mean our child's life had to be based on wishes also. This was happening.

Forgiveness, in my book, didn't offer a pardon and nor did it mean forgetting about any wrongdoing, but it did forgive him for what he knows not and me for being involved with him, giving me the consent to move on.

I held the belief that actions and behaviors are grounded in morals and values; most importantly, when no one is looking. Granted, I had made poor choices and didn't exercise good judgment for giving him the benefit of the doubt when doubt was screaming loud and clear, but that didn't resign me to have to be with Clyde.

I took a deep breath and began typing.

Dear Clyde,

As I have written in earlier emails, I have no interest in continuing a relationship with you. I understand that you are disappointed, but I am sure you will manage in time. Time heals all wounds, whether self inflicted or just inflicted. This shouldn't be about whether I forgive you. Forgive yourself and have the courage to change and you will heal. I do wish you well.

I need to share something with you, for no reason other than it's the right thing to do. I am a week late on my cycle and I have taken a pregnancy test and its positive. I have a doctor's appointment scheduled next week to confirm.

If you would like to discuss it, we can talk after you've had some time to gather your thoughts.

Best,

Olivia

I knew I had to get past this place of disregard with Clyde, but for now it was easier to immerse myself in my work and not think about it. I hit send.

I turned my attention to focus on the final touches to my presentation. My client was an Internet giant that was launching a social networking website. It was my job today to show its executives that if they chose me as their marketing representative, every aspect would be perfect. It was what I loved most doing: solving problems and coming up with creative solutions to a client's needs. My forte was all about every meticulous detail of the event and creating a great experience that each one of the attendees will remember.

My cell phone vibrated ten minutes later. Glancing at the caller ID, I saw that it was Clyde. I ignored the call, wanting to focus on the presentation. It was a conversation I wanted to have in private at home, not at the office.

By the time the presentation was done that afternoon, the three company executives returned from a ten-minute break, which felt like an hour, to inform me I'd won the deal. There'd be a follow-up meeting in a few days to execute the contracts to begin the launch over the next few months, planning every detail. Layla looked relieved. I glanced at my caller ID. Clyde had called twelve times.

I turned my phone face down on my portfolio. I was tense. I was normally ecstatic over landing a deal like this, but my thoughts were distracted to say the least.

"What's wrong?" Layla asked.

Before I could answer, the receptionist buzzed into the conference room. "Someone named Clyde is on the line for you. He says it's an emergency. He called ten times when you were in the meeting."

"Emergency?" Layla had a look of concern on her face. She got that look in her eyes when the school called about one of her kids.

I shook my head. "More like someone overdramatic." Layla still look concerned. "I'll take it in my office." I walked back to my office.

I closed the door, took a deep breath and picked up the receiver. "Hi, this is Olivia."

"You trapped me!" Clyde yelled.

"Believe me, Clyde, I want anything, but to trap you or to even see you." I spoke calmly. "I was just letting you know because it was the right thing to do."

"I don't want a baby!"

"I hear you, but it's not up to you," I said flatly.

"I don't want to be with you."

"Well, at least we agree on one thing." I looked out the window at the skyline.

"You're doing this alone and I want nothing to do with you."

"Then we agree, again," I said unemotionally.

He hung up. The sun was shining brightly.

Was I ready? I wondered after we hung up. *Would I be a good mom? Who would help me when the baby was sick or when work conflicted with caring for the baby? Would my breast milk come in? Did I even know how to change a diaper?*

I Googled 'How to change a diaper.' There were diagrams complete with instructions. I was good at following diagrams, especially with directions. I could do this. I was strong.

Reading my life backwards over the years, I concluded that things happened for a reason, and though I didn't always know what those reasons were and even took a few detours on my recognizance; my steps had been perfectly ordered and crafted with a purpose to learn and grow and to bring me to this exact place. I didn't want to dwell on why things happen, but trusted the reasons would be revealed in due time, knowing that God doesn't put more on you than you can bear. I was still standing. I could do this.

I was joyful for the transformation after a few weeks of learning I was pregnant.

Though I didn't think Clyde would necessarily be happy with or welcome my news, I did consider so many other ways a grown man could have responded to the news of having a child; a little less crass and with a little more reflection.

I resignedly admitted to myself…I wasn't good at picking good guys. I was just hoping to cut my losses and chalk the rest up to experience.

Three
FAITH

"SOMEBODY HAS FLOWERS," LAYLA SAID. "IT'S been a while, but clearly you've got someone's interest." She smiled, setting the bouquet of roses on my desk.

I opened the note.

Can you ever forgive me? I took the day off. I'm coming to town and would like to talk with you.

I took a deep breath; the aroma of the flowers overwhelmed me. I disliked roses. I disliked red roses most of all.

"Don't forget you have lunch for the Johnson account to recap the deliverables in an hour," Layla paused. "Who are they from?" She pointed, clearly seeing the blank look on my face. "The flowers?"

"Oh, no one. You're welcome to take them home or put them in the conference room." I glanced up from my computer. I wasn't ready to tell Layla.

"No one serious, you mean? I figured, since they're roses. Whomever he is, he doesn't really know you."

"Hey, Layla, how are the kids?" It wasn't that I wanted to change the subject, but I thought about how she managed everything. Her son was a straight honor student, a junior black belt in karate and took swimming and baseball lessons. Her daughter was in kindergarten and reading on a third grade level, took dance lessons, read music and often got the solo playing the piano. I wanted to tell her about the baby, but at ten weeks now, it was still too early to bring it up at work.

"They're great! Thanks for asking."

"I just realized I take so much interest in my clients and their lives, but I need to take more interest in the people around me, too. You've done an amazing job with your kids and I just wanted to tell you that."

"Thank you! God's done an amazing job with me. It's just my payback for all His blessings!"

"Amen to that!" I said quietly. "Alright, carry on with all you do." I ushered her away before getting sentimental. Pregnancy was already making me more sensitive. Some days, it felt like I cycled through every worry known.

By the time I returned from lunch, Clyde had left a message. My stomach instantly became unsettled as I listened to the voicemail. *Maybe it was the lunch,* I thought. "We need to talk about the situation, Olivia. I can't get you out of my mind. I'm in town, so let's meet for dinner and talk about our future." *It wasn't the lunch.*

In all the swirling emotions and confusion that I'd experienced over the past couple of months, one thing was clear to me: I wasn't interested in a future with Clyde, nor was I interested in hearing him try to convince me not to have my baby.

My disregard where Clyde was concerned increased as the day went on, but I knew I needed to call him back.

"Hello, Clyde. Before you start, please listen to me. This is not a situation, as you referred to it. I'm having a baby!" I declared. "I do recognize and accept that you will be the father of my child, but I am not interested in having a relationship with you. If you want to talk about how we'll manage going forward and you want to be in your baby's life, then we can talk."

There was a long pause.

"You had this all planned from the beginning!" Clyde shouted.

Rage began to escalate inside me. I stared at the wall, waiting for someone to wake me from this madness.

"I understand." I was diplomatic. "I would appreciate if I could get a family health history from you, if you would be so kind to provide it to me." I gathered my composure.

"Okay. I will, but we need to talk. Name a restaurant."

I hesitated. "Jaeger's downtown."

The last time I saw him was a few weeks before running into Randall on my flight to Charlotte. I swore I wouldn't ever see Clyde again. I felt numb.

Jaeger's had enough distractions when the conversation got dry with big screen televisions littered throughout the dining area, yet still dark enough for discreetness.

"No, thank you," I said for the third time, as he asked again if I wanted a drink. It was his fourth. It reminded me of the visits to Chicago. "I'm pregnant." I shook my head.

Clyde reached across the table and took my hands. Just touching him made me feel uneasy and sick to my stomach in a non-pregnant kind of way.

"Olivia, I think this happened for a reason. This can bring us back together. We're supposed to be in each other's lives. We can have kids later. Right now, you can spoil me. Right now, I'm not ready to share you with a child."

He leaned in to kiss me. I recoiled, pulling my hands away. "You mean you are not ready to share *you* with a child! You are such a narcissist! You think this pregnancy was meant to bring two people together that didn't need to be together in the first place, and this same pregnancy should be terminated to bring them back together? Are you serious or just crazy?" I paused. "Just so we're crystal clear on this. I am having a baby and not only do I not want you back, despite being pregnant by you, I don't want you back *because* I am pregnant!" Blood flowed through my veins, as my heart pumped stronger and faster with every beat. I was looking forward to my next run on the Greenway.

"So you made up your mind for both of us and I don't get a say?"

"This was never about you." I spoke quietly not wanting to draw any attention. "This isn't an ideal situation, and trust me when I say I am just as surprised to be having a child with you, but I'm going to do everything I can to be the best damn mother I can be, which includes doing what's best for my child. Starting now!" I stood, turning my back to him.

"Wait. You need to see this!" he said louder, as I started walking.

People were staring in a way people do when they're waiting to know what *it* is, almost open-mouthed like watching a thriller movie to find out whodunit, but don't want to appear too eager or nosey. They looked away when I caught their eyes.

I turned and looked back. He was holding up a piece of paper like a sign. Tears rolled down his face. The expression on his face didn't match. He looked proud. I had seen that look before on him.

I walked back to the table. The low light made it unable for me to make out the words from a distance.

DEATH CERTIFICATE. It read in bold letters cutting through the paper and through me. My knees weakened.

I took the document from him and sat down. *A child. Five months old. Cause of death: Multiple end organ failure.*

Clyde was nodding. "It was extensive organ malfunction. It tore my girlfriend and me apart when it happened. Losing a child felt like someone pulled out my heart while I was still breathing. It's genetic. Highly hereditary." He dropped his head dramatically, crying until he couldn't speak. A few staff members looked over at me, wondering if there was anything they could do.

I stared away, as my ears muted the background noise and my thoughts went immediately to my baby growing inside me. I was terrified. My mind raced to absorb the possibility of raising a child who might require extensive care; determined I'd get every possible genetic test available.

The gnawing feeling in my stomach was back and something was telling me something wasn't right. I didn't want to believe it. *This couldn't be happening.*

"There's more," he muttered. He sounded bold. I glanced up at him. His tears stopped. "I have a history of mental illness in my family. It's also hereditary." I sat motionless. He was quiet. A few tears appeared, as they glistened down his cheek in the dim light. "So you understand." He sounded absolute. It wasn't a question. It was a conclusion he had made. He reached for my hands again. I was limp. "There can't be a baby. Only me and only us." The tears were gone again.

After work, I spent hours at a time in the bookstore reading everything I could get my hands on for every stage of the baby's development and pregnancy. I was a research nut by nature. I read books about every mental illness and organ dysfunction and the possible signs of such in pregnancy. I was going through every worry known, though all my reading assured me it was normal given the hormonal changes I was going through. It meant I cared and that I was already putting someone else's needs first. Someone who undeniably was a blessing and who I would love unconditionally. Not to mention the emotional roller coaster I had been on.

The nights were harder in the silence, as it forced me to think about life with all the questions swirling in my head.

My friends were supportive, with at least one, but usually more calling me every day to check on me, while also encouraging me with kind words and sending care packages.

Running on the Greenway was my hour of unrequited time to think and visualize strength in my weakness like those wooden planks that held the weight as they became beaten down. As I breathed in air, I envisioned the muscles in my legs pumping blood to every cell in my body, as they exploded with energy, carrying me along on my stride.

God was opening another door for me, after it seemed another had been slammed shut.

Instead of dwelling on the past, I spent the present joining the local chapter of Parents Without Partners.

"Hello, we are so glad you could come. I'm Candace." A bubbly blonde with shoulder length wavy hair welcomed me at the door. I noticed she was impeccably put together, carrying an aura of energy. She had a gentle demeanor and her soft voice matched her five-foot-five-inch petite frame.

"Hi, thanks, I'm Olivia." I looked around. She stretched her hands out to receive mine. Even though I was here, I still felt awkward. I was an unwed, forty-year-old woman pregnant by a man that didn't want a child, and although it happens every day, certainly more often than society cares to recognize, there still very much exists a stereotype or judgment for being an unwed mother, for any reason, at any age.

"How old are your children?" Candace and I walked, as she told me about the offerings of the organization.

"Mine hasn't quite made it yet." I shyly patted my tummy.

"You're a planner like me. I love it." She giggled. "When is the blessed day?"

Candace smiled ear to ear seemingly reminiscing in her mind as we spoke. A few moments later, a pint-sized little girl, with strawberry blonde ringlets to her shoulders, grabbed Candace's leg.

"Speaking of… This is my little angel, Abigail." Candace placed her hand on top of her daughter's head.

"Hi, Abigail."

Abigail buried her face in her mom's leg.

"Abigail, this is Ms. Olivia. Say hello."

"Hi, Ms. Olivia," Abigail whispered. "Mom, can I go play some more?" Abigail hugged her mom's petite waist.

"She's precious," I said, watching Abigail as she ran off. "How do you keep it all together?" It was more rhetorical, but I asked for my sake, feeling overwhelmed.

Candace spoke calmly as she looked at me. "I think we're about the same age and we've lived long enough to learn that you can't change anyone else. I think I learned the hard way that when life gives you lemons, you just have to make lemonade." She paused. "Or you'll be bitter! Just remember to spit out the seeds!" She chuckled and looked away. Some kids were playing a game of dodge ball in the gymnasium. "Parenting is full throttle twenty-four-seven, three hundred and sixty five days every year. You have to draw your strength from within and I just didn't have time to figure out what her dad's problem was because I was too busy being a mom."

"Is it hard?"

"Oh God, yes! I can't lie, but it's also the most rewarding thing I've ever done." She sounded thankful. I could see it in her demeanor. I felt it in her voice.

On my drive home, I was distracted by the beautiful sunset, as evening began to set in. I decided to drive a little longer. The blue, orange and purple hues painted the sky with a wide airbrush, as though the artist released her bottled-up tension across her canvas scattered amidst the clouds ranging from darker angry hues to lighter shades where only weakness and peace remained in the upper atmosphere. I thought of sweet lemonade.

In the coming months, Candace and I became close friends. She was thirty-eight years old and had been in a relationship with a guy for a few years until—surprise—she got pregnant with Abigail. Candace's guy was happy and supportive in her pregnancy, until he learned he was having a girl. Candace kicked him out the next day when she was almost six months pregnant. She was also a breast cancer survivor and was laid off a month after her daughter was born while still on maternity leave. Her company ultimately closed down, giving her a nice severance package, and she relocated back to Charlotte to be closer to family.

A new city, a new baby and jobless, Candace seemingly broken, took a year off with her baby girl before she started getting her life back. The father of her child didn't make any contact with Abigail, except for the few pictures Candace had sent. She'd hoped it would change his heart for her child's sake, but over time when it didn't, she realized they were better off. From what I had seen, they were.

Relaxing on my chaise lounge, the subtle scent of jasmine incense filled the air. I inhaled deeply, as I thought of Candace. She inspired me. Or, in the least, I'd met someone who came from a common place. Like Layla. I had so much to learn from the many women that came before me. Woven from the same quilt in life, our pain has purpose when our prayers can focus on someone else's and you draw strength, faith and courage to your own. Stories of strength, love and forgiveness. All wanting to be a good parent.

My phone rang. It was Clyde.

"Thanks for taking my call. How are you?"

"Great. You?"

"Good considering."

Considering what? I thought. It always seemed as though Clyde's cup was somewhere between almost empty and drought dry, and he was the victim in everything. I wondered where this conversation would lead.

"I wanted to know if I could come to town to talk about where we go from here."

"I heard everything you had to say the last time you were here. I respect that you don't want to be a part of this, but I am having a baby and I'm not sure what else we need to talk about." I was tense as I clenched my jaw.

"That's just it. I've done some thinking and I want to talk about being a family."

Was I hearing things? I couldn't believe he said the 'F' word, as I choked on the water I was drinking. This guy didn't know family since *The Cosby Show* had been on television. *Maybe he's had a change of heart. Maybe he realizes a baby is something special.*

"Really? May I ask how that changed? Forgive me if I don't share the same sentiment that family is something you just decide to do. It's either who you are or it's not."

"Just hear me out and give me a chance," Clyde pleaded. "I didn't get to make the decision, but I can make this one now."

I listened. Something inside me wanted to believe him.

"I overheard somebody talking about a similar situation and they said it was the best thing to happen to them. I'd like another chance to do the right thing and try. Is it a boy or a girl?"

My ears heard what he said, thinking the creation of life surely should spawn some movement inside a person to want to try, but there was something gnawing inside me. Something that said he sounded rehearsed. Because he wanted to try would have helped me believe him, but not because he heard someone else did it.

"Are you there? Did you hear me?"

"Um, I don't know yet. I won't know the sex for a few weeks."

"I'll be there. Just say you will try. Say you'll let me try to be a father and I'll be there for you and the baby, and we can be together."

I was empty. "Clyde, I will never stop you from being your child's father, but I don't think we should be together. We weren't together before I found out I was pregnant and, even though it was unexpected, I don't think that means we should be together."

"You said 'think,' so there's still a chance. I'm just asking for that chance. I want to be a father because mine died when I was an infant. I can help you."

Could he? I wondered. *I need all the help I can get!*

"Think about it. You owe it to the baby to try."

"I don't think doing it for the baby is the right thing." I paused. *Is it? I want to do the right thing.* I felt guilty. "I really just want to focus on bringing my baby into this world healthy. Your decision can't depend on whether or not I am with you. You have to know what matters to you."

"This matters! I really want to raise my child!" He sounded enthusiastic. Dramatically enthusiastic and I just kept thinking performance.

I deliberated in my mind every minute of every day for the coming weeks, as I dug deep in my soul for what my conscience would allow me to live with. I didn't want my emotions to cloud my judgment. I wanted to do what was right, instead of having to be right.

I allowed guilt to creep in, while reluctantly convincing myself I had to give him the chance if he wanted to be a father. I didn't want to try or get back together, but I thought of my baby and the opportunity to grow up with a father. I had to give him credit for wanting to try. I owed my child that much. *Who am I to stand in the way of that?*

Over the next month, Clyde made a few trips to Charlotte to talk about how he could be around for the birth of his child, to help me and help raise our child. It sounded like a business proposal you could neatly tuck away in a box or an idea that was as fleeting as the wind. His plan was for me to move to Chicago since his practice was thriving, which might have made sense for someone you wanted to start your life with. *I did need all the help I could get. I could work remotely and travel for presentations and, since Clyde was willing to help, he could watch the baby while I traveled.*

As a child, I didn't fear change, even if it meant a subsequent change was necessary. I even thought I could control change. Now, as an adult, I was learning the difference between what I could and what I couldn't change.

Four
HOPE

MOVING IS STRESSFUL, WITH RELOCATING JOBS and packing
homes, but when you're moving into someone else's space, that's
a gross understatement. I agreed to move to Chicago since I could
relocate with the flexibility of telecommuting—at least until the
baby was born—and Clyde could be a part of his child's birth,
as he wanted. Being roommates was the only way I could afford
living in Chicago unless I considered a long commute living
outside the city, which I was not going to do with a new baby.
Clyde's assistance with the baby had to count for something.

I missed running on the Greenway—with all its imagery and
all the hope it represented from what it once was—where I could
reflect over my thoughts. The closest I'd come to recreating that
route, short of driving outside the city, was a route that wound
around the busy streets of the city and along the lake. I wanted
to keep running and not look back, although that would make

me have to admit all the poor choices I'd made; personally and professionally. I'd have to face my fears. I'd have to face my impatience and I'd have to face my pride.

It had only been three weeks since I moved to Chicago, but I had no idea how I was going to make it three more months to my due date.

It's one thing to date long distance and get accelerated weekend glimpses of best behavior, add a few glasses of wine and the conversation gets better, or at least it seems to. That is, until you realized the weekend glasses of wine also included daily drinks of vodka and cranberry, Bailey's chasers and Tom Collins that follow in the morning. The conversation, however, still did not get better.

Being in someone's space, you witness their mood swings and their gloom as their skeletons emerge from the darkness. Their presence is embedded in the walls. Their screams echo in the silence and their company is painfully obvious, even when you don't want to notice and try to drown out their voices with your own telling you to run.

Most nights, when Clyde was home, he did, basically, nothing, watching mindless adult swims shows staying up until the wee hours of the night doing who knows what.

The thought crossed my mind to hire a private investigator to quell my uncertainties before making any more decisions.

My child deserved truth and honesty, even if his father couldn't give that to me. I wanted to raise my child to be a considerate, honest and responsible young man, and knew the call upon my life was greater than having a baby. I was raising a human being, a son, a grandson, a friend, a brother, an uncle and one day someone's husband. Most importantly, I was raising a man.

God's gift to me was to birth my child safe and healthy into this world. My gift to God was to raise him up in a way he should go.

Contrary to Clyde wanting me to believe that his presence was critical to raising a boy, I had read that research says the bond between a mother and her male child is the single most beneficial bond in that male child's development, and a healthy mother-son bond has a direct correlation to a man's self-esteem and confidence. Research, I also read that speaks to a healthy bond between a father and son to the extent of identity, male patterned character and behavior.

I started meeting and mingling with the progressive and professional thirty-something and beyond crowd. That's when I met Trevor. Although the farthest thing from my mind was getting anyone involved in my drama, it didn't mean I couldn't have some much-starved-for intellectual adult conversation and some eye candy to admire in the process. Trevor had a majestic smile that would light up a room and it drew me in. He was every woman's knight in shining armor. Beyond his mocha-brown skin and big, dreamy, brown eyes, his statuesque build made me make a double take, as I noticed his presence. We were attracted to one another on sight when our eyes met and once we spoke, the chemistry was undeniable. I instantly felt he was more than just an attraction and I wanted to know him. He was a refreshing spirit that came in my life and I at least wanted the distraction for the time being.

We began meeting weekly for an after-work escape at the park or a coffee bistro to talk; it didn't matter where or for how long, as most nights were cut short because I didn't need any more conflict with Clyde or for him to suspect anything. When Trevor spoke, I felt comforted for hours and my soul began to crave hearing his voice. He would tell me I had the makings of the most beautiful creation and blessing ever and God found favor with me to bear that creation. Trevor would tell me that his purpose was to remind me of that. Daily.

We both wished for better timing and if God did have a sense of humor, I likened it more to being cruel and unusual punishment to meet a man like Trevor at a time like this. Maybe God's humor is simply an essence of His hope for things to come and to remind us that He always has ways we know not of. *Maybe this is a positive sign for me.*

"Hey, princess, are you running tonight?" Trevor called me one evening when he was leaving work at his law firm.

"Yes, of course. How's your preparation for your big deposition tomorrow?"

"I need to see you. I'll meet you there. I need to see you."

"Is everything okay?" I inquired with concern. "You are so good to me, Trevor."

"Yes, I'm fine. Until I know you are home, I won't be able to focus anyway." He paused. "Consider it protecting my interest." I could feel his smile.

"I know this is a lot for even a titan like you to shoulder. I'm carrying another man's baby and I think I may have found the man of my dreams." I confessed sadly before I realized I had verbalized my thoughts.

"You're pregnant? What?" I can't tell," he said sarcastically, and laughed. He always had a way of lightening the mood. "You've made me believe again and I want you to believe again, too, that there are still good men out here and I am one of them. I want to help you get through this." His voice was gentle. "I got you."

I was now smiling. "You are so good to me. Thank you for you! I'll see you later." *Maybe I could make better decisions.*

I prayed the reason Trevor was in my life was not only to see me through this season, but with any faith, it would be for a lifetime. Faith, after all, is the confidence of what we hope for will actually happen, and it gives us assurance about things we can't see.

I was faithful.

I stayed home from work to nest and sort, making room for the baby since Clyde had been as helpful as a sloth with the preparation, and I had grown tired of asking. I condensed the bookshelves, attempting some sense of order to make room for bins to house baby items from toys to toiletries. The things I had run across, not to mention the topics of books, pictures and other items were simply unmentionable.

Before meeting my girlfriends for our monthly book and dinner club, I set up to meet with a private investigator to exchange the necessary information.

Eli, the private investigator, was going to start following Clyde for a few weeks the next day when he left the office that evening. He would follow him at the office and the hospital for any midday departures and detours in the morning before and after work from home. We'd see where and how far that got us and if we needed to pursue or abandon the case from there. Clyde was vague of his routine and his schedule, so there wasn't much I could give Eli other than his office address, hospital privileges and staff names, the approximate time he left and returned home, the train he took, a picture, a couple of club memberships he mentioned to me in passing and a few names of friends.

Apparently, with a private investigator, a little goes a long way. I was quite intrigued that people have the occupation of revealing other people's secret lives and the methods they use. It was more exhausting to consider that people fabricate and lead second lives, maybe even more, and have to keep up with so much.

I was a little afraid for what may be revealed, but I needed to be sure and make better decisions so I could close this door without feeling guilty, even though all the answers I needed were already seeded in my doubt.

"Why did you do that?" Aunt Ernestine asked. I called her on my walk home from the track. I used the twenty-minute walk to catch up with friends and family for privacy.

"I have to know because this guy is going to be my son's father, and I want to know if I should move back to Charlotte." I wanted her to stop the questions since I already had a lot of my own, and didn't have the answers to hers or mine.

"Hope, this is not like you. Just drop him and move on. What do you possibly have to know that you don't already know that will help you decide whether to leave or not? Isn't your suspicion your answer?"

"I'm just doing my research because I'll have to interact with this guy the rest of my child's life, and I have to protect my child."

"I trust you and if you are in danger, you will tell me. By the way, I met your friend, Candace, at one of the centers I work at in the community. She's such a nice girl, and her daughter is darling. We exchanged numbers to keep in touch. She asked how you were doing." I was relieved she changed the subject because I did not want to field any more questions.

"They are great! Candace and her daughter are darling, aren't they? I have to reach out to her and catch up. Now that I think about it, you are both very similar, which is why I love you both. I'm so happy you both met." I was smiling. "The universe is incredible; how it is all intertwined and such a small world."

"Yes it is. Listen, sometimes you just have to know when it's time to cut your ties and run"

"Oh my gosh, Ernie, I just had a déjà vu. That's what the marriage counselor told me when I was married to Jack. This guy makes him look like a saint!" I sighed, looking to the sky. "Just covering my bases this time. Things always work out even when they make no sense." I felt a lump forming in my throat.

Clyde never met Aunt Ernestine for a reason. Mostly because we weren't serious for me to introduce him to my people, but also I knew she would have seen right through what I made excuses for. The sky was clear, as the evening sun was beginning to set.

"He's not your worry. Only that baby of yours is. Remember what I always say; listen and silent have the same letters." Ernestine was in her mid-fifties and didn't look a day over forty.

"Ernie, I'm getting excited to meet my baby! I'm almost home." The tension was growing inside me, as I came around the corner of the next street over from home.

"Well, you're my Hope and I know you and your baby will come out of this just fine. I love you." I could feel her smile over the phone. Her words warmed me.

"I love you, too, Ernie!"

Feeling the comfort of her words, I wanted to skip the last block home. The single thing I loved about her was that she told it straight like it was and was always willing to listen. She was a strong woman and, although she wasn't my biological aunt, she was close like one; or what I imagined one would be like. Mine lived across the globe. We met at a soup kitchen almost seven years ago in Charlotte, but it had been more than ten years since the accident.

Her husband and their two young children left the house one evening to get ice cream and never returned. A drunk driver crossed the median and hit them head on, causing their vehicle to roll. Even buckled in, the kids were killed instantly with the impact and her husband died before the ambulance could reach the hospital. She was relieved knowing he did since she knew the pain would have tormented him, but she always wished she could have hugged them one more time. In the few years that followed, she indulged in excessive alcohol, followed by a few more years of anger and isolation for a few more years until she broke down. Sadness and grief filled her, and soon after, she gave her life to God again. Now, Ernestine volunteers at every organization known, every minute she is able.

She was withdrawn when I met her, but carried a light of strength when she approached me one day. She told me there was something about my energy that offered her hope, as she opened up in that moment, sobbing gently as she spoke. There were no tears. Her face was expressionless. Only pain and emptiness remained. I will never forget that moment when we met.

I was the first person she told about the accident and, from that day forward, she named me Hope, thanking me for giving her a way forward. The irony was that Ernestine gave me hope and we were two bruised souls that the universe so kindly allowed to cross paths. I watched her offer compassion and patience to everyone that came to the center. I felt guilty for being overwhelmed with my seemingly simple dilemma as I witnessed her selflessness.

Earnestine never wanted pity from anyone and believed she was spared to do God's work, to make a difference on others' journey and she always gave her best. She made me determined to always give mine.

Funny how people on the outside can call things after just a few short interactions with people, but when you are close to a situation, you can't tell your left from your right. I was happy I was on the way out and not stuck without a place to go.

Dr. Alson, my Obstetrician, was born and raised in Detroit and, like a well-traveled big sister, would fight my battles no matter that I tried to be the tough girl. She would tell me that life's battles aren't meant to be fought alone and gave me more courage with every visit, advising me as if I were one of her own. Maybe she saw it a lot. Maybe she lived a lot. I was just thankful for her.

"Did you decide about my offer?" Dr. Alson asked, as she entered the exam room, closing the door behind her. She was average height with the athletic build of a swimmer. Today her hair was pulled back in a single loose ponytail.

"Thanks for offering your townhouse, but I just think I should stay put since I don't know anyone or my way around the city. And, I am so close to delivering." I dropped my head, feeling ashamed for choosing to stay. I was more ashamed for being here and thinking this arrangement with Clyde could work in the first place. "I've never had to depend on anyone."

Dr. Alson put her hand on my knee and shook it gently, motioning me to lie down. "I'm not judging you for anything and you don't have to be afraid because you have friends that love you and want to help. Do you think it would help if Roger spoke to him, so he understands he shouldn't do anything stupid between now and then?" She looked directly at me through her thick-rimmed eyeglasses resting on the tip of her nose, as if she wanted to see inside my eyes rather than hear me respond with my mouth. She squeezed the cold gel on my belly. I jumped, feeling uncomfortable. Not from the cold gel, but because I was uncomfortable with the reality of my life.

Dr. Alson knew the plan and advised me to remain in Chicago until my child was three months old and we were both healthy and strong before moving.

"I don't know if it's worth the confrontation with his temper and ego. I've seen how big your husband is, and Clyde is no match." I chuckled.

Maybe it was growing up in another country, which was less of the 'what can you do for me' and more of the 'live and let live' mentality, and being a late bloomer of sorts that made me want to believe people were generally good and kind at their core. Or, maybe it was not involving myself in much drama in my childhood—at least not of this magnitude—that made me mildly naïve, albeit by design, because of my disdain for crazy. Ignorance is bliss; I'm sure in whole because of my strict upbringing that limited the time spent hanging out with friends, keeping us busy with extracurricular activities with not much time for much else to get involved in. I wasn't necessarily prepared with street smarts, but common sense always guided me and my conscience was grounded in the right place. That's the irony of common sense. It's not that common.

"Okay, but you have my cell phone if you change your mind. It's currently vacant, so you can move in any time." She connected the monitor and turned on the sound, as she glided the instrument over my belly. "Sometimes life allows things to happen, good and bad, to mature a person and make them stronger and wiser to face the blessings ahead. After all, life is about the journey and not the destination, and you will have a greater appreciation for all of this. I promise." I wanted to believe her.

I rested in that simple insight, already envisioning life on the other side, knowing with each day I was one day closer to freedom, as I awaited the arrival of my baby.

"Thank you!" I looked away ashamed. I didn't want to think about how I got to this place.

"It's very strong. Do you hear it?" Dr. Alson changed the subject, taking a few measurements. She was nodding with a look of approval. I was relieved.

I heard it over the speaker. *Thump thump, thump thump, thump thump...* It sounded like it was in stereo, making my heartbeat louder and we were in unison. I smiled, watching his image across the monitor. It wasn't the first time I had heard the heartbeat or the first time I saw his tiny image, but this time I saw him so clearly.

"There he is," I whispered. My eyes began to tear; thankful my pregnancy was progressing smoothly. Dr. Alson cleaned my tummy with a paper towel and turned off the machine.

Sitting on a stool, Dr. Alson pushed herself away from the exam table. "There are no signs of distress and the measurements are right in line with our due date. We have a few months to go. Keep doing what you are doing and elevate those legs at nighttime. It will help reduce the swelling as the weather gets hotter also." She resumed her professional manner. "Listen to your body with the running and drink lots of water."

"I will. I feel good." I hesitated. "And…I met someone," I blurted out.

She smiled. "There's a happy ending for you. I know it! You are a good person, Olivia. Be careful and take things slow. And, for the record, I have no patience for narcissists that have the nerve to ask how much time a baby needs." I believed her. "Clyde is very selfish. You're doing great. I'll see you in a few weeks. Call me if you need anything." I stood up and she put her hand on my forearm, stopping me. "Anything!"

I nodded in confirmation.

My family also knew the plan because I didn't want them to be concerned; namely my dad, knowing I'd have to sell my jewelry to get him out of jail.

"We're not together, so why do you care?"

I couldn't believe it had only been six short weeks. Clyde had shown me whom he was after begging me to move halfway across the country in the name of 'trying.'

"Please don't play the victim anymore and act like you are trying so hard to win me back. We're going to be parents and it would be nice if we could be honest with each other, at least until I leave."

"I am being honest." He darted around the apartment like a lost chicken without any particular direction. Clyde was home early that day, claiming he didn't feel well. "Now you're leaving?"

"I just can't believe someone doesn't know where they got symmetrical bruises on their knees," I ignored his inquiry. "And they're still red."

Clyde walked to the bathroom to look in the mirror. Bending down, he looked at his knees. "I don't see them, but whatever you think you see I don't know where they came from," he said dismissively, as he continued to dart from room to room. "I swear on a stack of Bibles."

His stare was brazen. I got a chill down my spine, thinking of his callousness for making such claims, especially since I had never heard him say a prayer, much less go to church. His eyes looked like hollow cesspools and it became painstakingly clear that Clyde's conscience did not exist. He was empty.

Five
LIES

⊶

"HOW HAVE YOU BEEN?" WALTER ASKED when he called.

"I'm good. Few months to go and heartbeat is strong. I've got a fighter!" I was breathing hard, as I finished my run. "Oh, and Clyde showed up with bruises on his knees, but he doesn't know where he got them." I slowed to a walk. The early evening was still hot.

A mutual friend introduced me to Walter a few years ago and we clicked instantly. He was handsome and funny and a good person to his core. Walter treated me like a queen and we dated soon after meeting for almost a year until I selfishly decided I didn't want the ready-made family with two young children. He was newly divorced and made it known he had no desire of having more children. I backed out gracefully because I wasn't ready to trade my option of having children for a man that had unilaterally given his up. Even though our relationship took a different course, we remained friends and still confided in one another in most matters of life, personally and professionally. I appreciated his tell-it like-it-is personality, much like my own and his wit was definitely step-to-step with mine.

"How does someone not know where they get bruises on their knees? They're called carpet burns. He must think you are stupid if he thinks you wouldn't know. Bruises on your knees are kind of obvious. Are you running?"

"Just finished. And, they were still red, so it would have been fairly recent. Can we talk about something else?" I didn't want to revisit the fact that I had made another bad decision that was now staring me in the face. I had enough on my mind, thinking about my exit plan. It was about time I had one.

"Maybe someone worked him over." He laughed. I missed his laugh and his smile.

"WALTER!" I said loudly, looking around me. I continued to walk up and down the streets, taking the longer way home. My heart rate was almost to resting.

"I'm just saying. I just don't get it. You're pregnant and moved across the globe to allow him to witness his child's birth and he could have had the chance to really clean up his act and try to be together. Have you met any of his friends?"

"Sure, the people he wants me to meet, but it's contrived. No one knows he's friends with the other, even though they all went to school together." *Maybe if I had introduced Clyde to my friends they could have warned me,* I thought.

"He's just bizarre." He sounded as puzzled as I felt. I stopped to stretch on the footbridge overlooking the lake.

"He is, and I see it so clearly now. He wavers between the hard-on-his-luck good guy just looking for a break to the big doctor living it up, accruing debt in the Windy City. And, there's also the round-the-way guy that's hip to the culture." I rubbed my belly, feeling a little tight, but invigorated.

"He's just bizarre!"

"You said that already."

"Okay, he's shady, but I'm trying to make sense of him and I just can't put the two of you together. Did you ever talk to any of the friends about him?"

"No, that's not me, but ironically, a few sought me out to warn me about him." I resumed my walking.

"Really? His friends warned you about him? That should've been a sign." The statement pierced me. *Another bad decision.* "I'm exhausted just listening to you. I don't know how you stayed!"

"I know. I know. Well, I'm done now. I'm just happy to know I'm not crazy or hormonal like he wants me to think." I took a deep breath, feeling my muscles loosen as I breathed in.

"Well, wonder no more. The guy lies when he doesn't even have to. That's pathologic *and* tiring!"

"Ya think? I feel so stupid," I said abruptly. My words stabbed me.

"Sounds like this guy has been doing this a long time. Just take the lesson and that blessing growing inside you. Enough about him, how are you feeling these days? You're gonna have that baby while you're running!" We both laughed.

"Well, I hope the baby and God can both forgive me. I'm so stressed, but running helps me cope."

"Is that good for the little guy?"

"Not sure about the baby, but I know it's good for me. Doc says it's fine since I always did it." I smiled as a passerby gave me thumbs up.

"So how are the moving plans coming?"

"All prelim at the moment, but I filled out the application and got approved for the townhome. I have only seen it online, so when time gets closer, I'll probably want you to do a walk-thru and pick up the keys for me." I shook my hair out from under my baseball cap. I felt the light breeze against the sweat dripping on the back of my neck.

"Olivia, I'll help you any way I can! You're my girl," Walter replied in his southern drawl. Born and bred, and never left. It comforted me. I was thankful for Walter.

I began my walk back home.

It had been a hot summer in Chicago and Clyde's apartment only had a window A/C unit. I guess I didn't ever expect Chicago to be so hot, growing up just north, but I also had never lived without central A/C either, not to mention the added thirty pounds that had my temperature climbing and my heart racing.

My life had become toxic. I was in desperate need of change, feeling isolated on the nights I didn't see Trevor. Most mornings,

I left for work before Clyde even woke up. I'd cook dinner in the evening and then head out to run or vice versa, and if I didn't do either, I'd take a detour after work to catch up with Trevor. Many days I wouldn't even go into the office, circling back home after knowing Clyde had left, spending the day doing whatever I fancied. I'd try new restaurants and explore new areas of the city, treating myself to the spa almost weekly. The days I did go to work, I looked forward to my hour commute as time to sort through my thoughts and listen to the latest radio talk show drama to escape my own. Although, most days it seemed as though someone peeked into my life and overheard the conversations in my head. Conversations that told me to run and not look back.

It didn't matter to me what Clyde did and nor did I inquire, not wanting to field any questions about my whereabouts and risk losing my newfound freedom. I'd fabricate stories of back pain, swollen feet, tiredness and discomfort or any excuse to go to bed early to avoid interaction, doing just enough to keep the peace.

I kept a daily planning log of what needed to be done to finalize the move back to Charlotte. Since I was going to take a leave of absence and I worked mainly on commission for the accounts I brought in, the relocation would be on my dime and figuring my budget was high on the list.

Some people learn the hard way, while others learn the long way. I was learning the long hard way, but I knew my faith, my belief and my trust would get me back on my feet again. I had survived a fatal attraction and a near fatal car accident earlier in my life, and trusted that God didn't bring me through those experiences to allow this one to happen for any other reason than to prevail just the same.

⮐

Eli, the private investigator, and I planned to meet one afternoon after two weeks of following him. He told me he had what he thought was enough information to share and what he thought was disconcerting and disturbing.

From the suit he described he'd be wearing, I spotted Eli sitting in the corner of the bar of the W Hotel lobby, watching ESPN Sports. He was tall and handsome. His salt and pepper hair gave him a very distinguished look. Trevor recommended Eli as having been in the business many years and being meticulously thorough and discreet, and for having some scandalous cases that he was able to unveil. He smiled as our eyes made contact, as I approached him.

"Wow, Olivia, Trevor told me you were pregnant, but you don't look like you are about to have a baby or be anyone's mother, for that matter." Eli stood up and extended his hand. I felt myself blushing, remembering my neatly tucked basketball in my tummy that identified me.

"Thanks, Eli. I appreciate your ability for great damage control and compliments when you are the bearer of bad news. I like that!" I chuckled. I sensed a cool nervousness about him. Perhaps because of the possible implications of the news he had to share with me.

"Do you want to move over to the couches and be more comfortable?" He stretched out his arm. I noticed his muscular, athletic build as his suit jacket opened away from his torso. "Would you like some juice, cheese?" Eli looked back at the bartender for service.

"I think I would. How did you know I was craving cheese? And, some fruit would be wonderful, too, if they have some, please. Thanks." I wandered over to the couch near the large palladium windows overlooking Lakeshore Avenue and Lake Michigan. The lobby bar was scarce with just a few patrons. It was still early evening.

"By the way, I love cheese, so I was hoping you would want some and it sounded like a craving thing." Eli joined me on the couch. "Olivia, I'll jump right in because I know you need to go. If you have questions, stop me any time, but I will explain what I have done and what I also discovered." Eli's voice became more official. His words stabbed me. *Discovered? Maybe this was a bad idea.* I stared at him for any possible facial expression. He had hazel eyes and his facial bone structure indicated a mixed heritage of African American with either Persian or Italian descent. His skin was brown and smooth.

"You mean more like what you uncovered in my case?" I smirked.

"Ah, beautiful and witty."

"Just trying to cut the very thick air. I'm sorry, I've just never hired someone to tell me the person I'm involved with, let alone the father of my child, has been lying. I'll just have to deal with whatever you tell me and find a way to manage my disgust, judging by your very professional tone." I was restless, and tried to find a comfortable position on the deep pillow couch that swallowed me in when I sat down. "What you tell me is going to help me move on and close this book of my life." I was convinced. "You can tell me everything and I'll be okay with it. Really, I mean that!"

A young lady brought a small cheese and fruit plate, two glasses with a pale fruit juice, two more with water and some napkins.

"Good attitude. Something tells me you've already moved on and looking at you, you will be just fine. More than fine. Trust me! Okay, let me get down to it." He popped a cheese square in his mouth. "I was able to follow Mr. Walters to and from work and home, as well as a few extended absences from work in the middle of the day a few days a week. I assume on his surgery days. I followed him a total of ten days over the past two weeks, and I think there's enough information of what I think you are looking for, and more time would probably be more of the same." He looked at me for some outward reaction. There was none. I was relaxed. I felt safe. "I am not sure what he tells you, but given you hired me, you already know he is probably not where he says he is or doing what he says he is doing." I nodded, feeling queasy not knowing what I was about to hear. "I have to say, and I've been doing this eleven years and have some pretty raunchy and scandalous cases and I've seen more than I cared to, that he's one of the most predictable people I've had to follow and he actually made it easy for me. He's a creature of habit and he's clueless to the world around him, although he tries to appear covert. Just my observation, but there may be a twist and that's the disturbing part I mentioned." Eli's manner seemed almost numb, but concerned. Maybe he was numb since he'd been doing it for some time and seen so much.

"I hired you for a reason and I don't think I'll be surprised." I stared off, reminding myself this was a good thing and that I had to do it.

"Most, if not all, from what I could tell, his meetings were not professionally related and he prefers one-on-one interactions because he likes to be in control, as well as get all the attention. He has a persona of a narcissist, but that's pure observation." *I thought it before having heard the word, but never understanding what it meant. My doctor tagged it immediately after talking with Clyde and now Eli on sheer observation.* I reached for some fruit, distracting my thoughts. I felt numb inside.

"I have two sets of pictures, but I don't think you need them unless you want them." There was a long pause. Everything seemed quiet in the background. I didn't hear the hum of the vents. I didn't hear the television. "Olivia, Clyde does spend a considerable amount of time with other women. No one person in particular, and not even a particular type that stands out, which is interesting on a primitive level and his modus operandi is nothing short of a man on a quest, which is classless, but he's successful at least fifty percent of the time, which keeps him out there. He moves fast, he's superficial and he comes across rehearsed. And he's very self-consumed. I think his lack of discretion and his indiscriminate choices explains the next part." Eli was looking at me again for any reaction. There still was none.

I sat motionless, listening, eating cheese and sipping my juice. I was thinking of my moving plans. There were a few more customers sitting at the bar now.

"Are you okay?"

"Yes." I was flat.

"Clyde also spends a considerable amount of time with men. Their interaction seems to be more than male bonding and they met more than once over the two weeks. Olivia, I need to ask you this. Do you think Clyde is..."

"What? No!" I cut Eli off. I was uncomfortable.

"I mean has he ever said anything or done anything that made you think that..."

"Absolutely not! I think I would know that." I paused. I was at a loss for words. "I mean a woman would know. Did you see anything?" My belly felt tight from the inside.

"Nothing specific, but some awkward body language."

"Oh my gosh, no. I would know." I dismissed the thoughts. "I mean, I know I hired you because I didn't know some things, but that I'm pretty sure I would know." My body was numb. My thoughts recalled to when Clyde became extremely defensive when I inquired about his whereabouts, thinking it was hardly the response one would expect from a person that did not have to defend his faithfulness.

"Are you okay?"

"Yes, just distracted for a moment. You confirmed my suspicions regarding other women and I'm not surprised in the least with anything you are telling me. That's why I hired you, although I was hoping I was wrong. Forgive me if I have nothing to say." I glanced out the windows at the expressionless people passing by. *Or, maybe I was the one projecting how I felt.*

"You're a smart woman. Don't deny yourself that. There is nothing to understand when someone cheats, and you did the right thing by coming to me when you started to suspect something. He probably played like you were oversensitive or emotional, being pregnant." He stared blankly at me. "I'm not going to read about any homicides in Hyde Park in the Tribune tomorrow, am I?"

I laughed. "This is not my battle. I am not that person and that's one guarantee I can make! I held up my end of the bargain, being here, and I can assure you when I have my baby, I will also have all the necessary health screening tests done." I wanted to cry, but no tears would come.

"Good girl! You can have the pictures and you never know when you may need them. I have a few suggestions for their use, but I would be wrong for even suggesting it, but be careful how you use these, if you so choose." Eli handed me the envelope. I raised my arm to meet his. Looking at the cheese and fruit now made me nauseous. I looked away.

I moved to the firmer cushioned chair opposite Eli. "Unbelievable!" I exhaled, changing the subject.

"Olivia, guys who cheat are only cheating themselves because they are denying themselves true happiness. I'm not sure if they're just lost, but they are dangerous to everyone, especially themselves with sexually transmitted diseases and HIV/AIDS. They are reckless and it is really out of control these days.

"I gave him the benefit of the doubt. I just wanted honesty."

A different cocktail waitress, with an upbeat energy, appeared inquiring if we needed anything. Eli asked for more water and gestured to me. I noticed she never took her eyes off him. I shook my head and looked out the window. The rush hour crowd was thinning.

"You gave him the benefit of the doubt, but in truth, when we do that, we are just doubting ourselves. The majority of us probably do that because we want to believe people are good. You put it together fairly quickly though, so don't cut yourself short."

"It was only a few months and I was already pregnant."

"And you said it was long distance, which tends to also accelerate things and even though you didn't get to see his day-to-day life before you moved, you still figured it out. You should be an attorney or a detective." Eli tried to console me, but it felt more like a dagger, reminding me that I didn't follow my intuition.

"I've heard more than I care to know and I don't have the stomach for this type of drama to make a life of it." I laughed. "About the only drama I want to be around these days are diaper changes and sleepless nights."

He smiled. "I hear you. You have to remove yourself from it or you become jaded, but I do it because I want to help good people like you." He smiled. "I still can't believe you're having a baby. Like any day now, right? Did you tell me boy or girl? Do you have a name picked out?" Thankfully, he changed the subject.

"You're great for a pregnant woman's ego. About four weeks to go and I'm having a boy. I haven't officially picked out a name yet, but that's another story. I have a lot of those stories. I know one thing. I sure can't make them up." I chuckled. The reality of my life now sadly resembled a drama-meets-horror movie.

"No you can't! Trevor told me you were a strong woman, but now hearing your story, I see it! Your guy will reap what he's sown! I'm just glad you got the answers you need to move on. Do you think you are in any type of danger when you confront him?" His tone switched to concern.

"No. I'm not going to confront him. The best thing for him to do would be to let me go quietly. There are too many people that know my story that he'd be the first person they'd look for. He should want me gone."

"You're a smart woman. Did you say you were moving to Charlotte?"

"Yes. I was there before I moved here." Eli nodded his head; distracted in his own thoughts.

"What a small world. I used to live in Charlotte and still have some friends out there. My aunt moved there years ago. I get there kind of regularly. I'm due for a trip, in fact. It's a small world." He was still distracted by something like he was calculating in his mind.

"I was just telling someone the same thing the other day. I have to wait until after the baby's born before we can move. Speaking of moving, I better get out of here and catch at least a short run to quell this stress you just caused me." I chuckled, looking outside as the sun was beginning to set. I glanced at my watch.

"You're still running?" Eli was surprised. "IN-credible!"

"It's the only thing that keeps me sane, Eli. I'm not all that incredible. It's my therapy. Besides, I want this baby to be proud of his mom." I was humbled.

"Are you kidding? Call me when the baby is here and I'll tell him myself what you went through and he'll be proud!" We stood. "I just met you, but I am already so proud of you! Which train do you need to catch?" Eli looked over his shoulder at the street outside.

"The Metra Electric at McCormick Place, but I've got to run to the restroom before I do." I patted my tummy.

"I need to catch the Red Line to Lincoln Park. Trevor would want me to make sure you got on your train and me as well. I'll wait and we can walk together."

Eli was looking out the lobby doors, finishing up on his cell phone when I returned from the restroom.

"Ready?" I said from behind him.

"Yes." We talked more, as we walked and bid our good-byes when we reached the platform. Reaching out for a hug, his chest and shoulders seemed to envelope me. "Be safe and call me if you need anything."

Six
JOY

I GOT HOME WITH ENOUGH TIME to change and get to the track before the sun would be going down. Trevor met me there and we were going to grab a quick bite afterwards. Distracted in my thoughts, we didn't exchange too many words and decided to cut our run short. Trevor waited in the cab downstairs while I took a quick shower, pulled on a black sundress with sandals and returned. I wanted to see Trevor. He always had a way of comforting me, without ever having to say a word.

"Listen, I know you don't want to talk much, but we can go to my place and order something there and just relax if you don't feel like being out. It's your call." Trevor was quiet, as he opened his hands to hold mine.

"I think I'd like that. I don't want to be out." I was flat.

"Michigan and East Pearson," he told the cabbie, sitting back in the seat.

"I just wanted to see you. I like Eli. Did I say thanks for the referral?" I smiled, nestling under his arm, as he pulled me closer. I felt safe.

"Shhhhh. Just relax. I got you," Trevor whispered, kissing my forehead. "How's the prince doing?" Trevor changed the subject gently, while he rubbed my tummy. He always had a way of changing the subject at just the right time, when I hoped he would. "Did I tell you that's a great dress?" He lifted my chin with his fingers to look at me.

"No, you didn't." I smiled, poking him in his side. "Thanks, T." The cab ride was quick and it was quiet. Climbing out, I looked around and saw that we were off Michigan Mile at a high rise beside the Ritz Carlton hotel.

"We can order something from the hotel restaurant and they'll bring it up." He held his hand out for me, leading me inside to the elevators. As we stood, Trevor held me close, as I rested my head on his chest. The elevator chimed, as it came to a rest. "Twentieth floor," the electronic voice said.

Swinging the door open, he gestured me to enter. "Welcome to my home, Olivia." He was always a gentleman. My eyes were drawn to the floor-to-ceiling windows, with a view overlooking the city, with Lake Michigan in the distance and the night lights that lit the dark sky. "Make yourself at home." Jazz music played over the surround system. "We can order off the computer. It usually takes about twenty minutes."

"The view is breathtaking!" Walking toward the windows, I was mesmerized. "He's been cheating," I blurted out casually, looking back at Trevor.

The expression on his face told me he was searching for an appropriate response. There was none. He stepped behind me and intertwined his arms under mine, wrapping them around me firmly. "How do you feel?"

"I can't say I'm surprised, but I just want to get as far as I can away from him. Why me?" My eyes started to tear as I stared out the window. "I mean, I'm okay with being a single mom, but why does the father of my child have to be this guy?"

"Hey, hey, baby girl. Blessings come through you, not to you and God chose you to bless." Trevor spoke slowly, as he turned me around to face him, pressing his finger against my lips.

"I don't know what I would have done without you these last few months. I appreciate you. I just wish our timing were different. It feels so nice to be with a man that respects and cherishes me." I sniffled, laying my head on his chest.

"Shhhh. Everything is going to be fine. And, don't forget this man cares about you. You are strong and you inspire me." Lowering himself to look in my eyes, he touched his forehead to mine. Trevor stood six feet three inches. "Hey, let's order. You need to feed the prince." He changed the subject. As always, perfectly timed.

I followed Trevor to the kitchen where a screen displayed the menu offerings. While Trevor showered, I reclined on the couch looking at the lights of the city glowing in the darkness. The music played softly in the background.

"Do you want to lay down?" Trevor asked quietly. I must have dozed off after eating.

"I think I do and my feet are swollen like little pillows."

Reaching out his hand, he led me to his bedroom. I stopped at the threshold. "Wait, I'm not sure about this."

He chuckled. "I'm not going to touch you…well, unless you want me to, that is." Trevor flashed a smile. "I want you to stretch out and relax and get some sleep. I got you."

I know you do. I'm pregnant with another man's baby and I've got a big belly and…"

"Yes. You mentioned that before. I'm here because I want to be here and I love you being here with me. I'm not going anywhere. I want to be here for you." My head hung. I was embarrassed for thinking more. Maybe it was my thoughts to want to feel the loving emotions that should accompany a pregnancy that my body and heart yearned for. I wanted to feel close to him. He gently held me away to look at me. "Lay down and let me rub those little pillows….I mean, feet." He smiled. I felt safe and took a deep breath.

I sat on the edge of the bed, as Trevor rubbed my feet slowly. He raised my feet to rest on his chest as he stood. I lay back on the bed. I watched him as he watched me and felt his energy. I began to feel warm and closed my eyes. I wanted to feel his touch.

"Are you okay?" I woke, a little disoriented where I was. I felt the soft, warm sheets on my skin. Trevor enveloped me from behind as we lay on our sides. "You fell asleep and I tucked you in," he whispered.

"Thank you." My body was relaxed. My mind was exhausted. "Are you?" I reached my arm behind me to hold him across his waist.

"You are beautiful and amazing!" He stroked my belly. A peace came over me. "I am doing perfect and I am perfect for you." I felt a kiss on the nape of my neck. My body felt warm.

In the next few weeks, I was growing more and more uncomfortable, feeling every single change they explained in childbirth class. From the baby descending and getting in position to the widening of my pelvic bones, although it felt more like my pelvis being pulled in opposite directions by a crane. It was happening. I grew a lot more nervous with every bit of excitement.

Some days were easier than others, but the stress living with Clyde certainly didn't help. I couldn't stand being in his space and I couldn't even stand to look in the mirror at myself for being there. I longed to be with Trevor every minute I could get away. I missed his smell and his touch.

The news Eli delivered a few weeks prior slowly wore inside me, although I tried as much as I could to deny that it affected me. I believe disgust had set in after a warm bath one evening, as I began to have sharp pains and feeling pressure stronger than I had ever felt before. I was exhausted, hoping the pain would subside to go to sleep.

When I told Clyde I was having contractions, he grudgingly loaded up the car for the hospital. I had interrupted his watching something on television. The nurse called the false alarm after taking one look at me and we returned home. With two more weeks remaining, I grew more and more anxious.

I garnered the energy to run very slowly the next morning and wobbled to my doctor appointment afterwards. I was dilated a centimeter and time was indeed near. Although my doctor didn't expect I would make it the remaining two weeks to my due date, she did estimate at least another week to go as I still had nine more centimeters to dilate. I was saddened because I wanted the clock to start ticking until I would be able to move.

That night I wrote in my journal before settling to bed, with my feet elevated on some pillows. Feeling sharp, stabbing pains in my lower abdomen, I was immediately paralyzed from my legs down. *Surely, my doctor knows a week when she sees one*, I thought. The pain subsided for about four minutes until another stabbing pain followed, with even more intensity. I called a car service to take me to the hospital since Clyde had been out that evening. I text messaged him to meet me at the hospital. If I were wrong again, I'd push the baby out myself so I didn't have to hear Clyde complain that it was another false alarm and I could start my countdown. Even though I had wished for labor to come, I didn't expect my contractions to be only two minutes apart. *Careful what you wish for. This time, it is time.* I had experienced pain from broken bones from my car wreck and was not given painkillers for eight hours, but in retrospect, that pain now seemed like a mosquito bite. *It is true what they say about labor pains that you know when you know,* I thought. I knew. It was time.

As fate would have it, Dr. Alson was the attending OB on call that evening at The University of Chicago Medical Center. I was relieved, not having met the doctor with the prior false alarm. When Clyde arrived, Dr. Alson asked Clyde to leave the room, so we could briefly discuss my plan before things got harried, to say the least, with a new baby and moving. Her calm disposition centered and prepared me for what I was about to endure.

"Don't allow yourself to be disturbed by Clyde anymore. Focus your energy on the plan God has for you and this baby." She spoke deliberately. "He can't hurt you anymore unless you allow him to." It sounded like a pep talk. I needed one.

I nodded as I began to cry. I was relieved and scared.

Dr. Alson advised me to get plenty of rest in the coming months and suggested about bonding as much as I could with the baby. Concerned for the baby's safety and health, Dr. Alson wondered whether Clyde was capable of caring for a baby since he was too selfish to care about anyone else.

"It will still be two to three hours before you'll be dilated enough to be ready to labor." Dr. Alson patted my arm.

I felt another contraction and clenched my jaw, as she spoke. My focus was waning.

"I need you strong and rested to labor. When you are rested, the chances for better latching with breastfeeding after birth are greater and the first five minutes are critical for good bonding."

She spoke intentionally and slowly for me to understand the consequences of what she was telling me. "If you want an epidural, now is the last chance for us to do that and you can take a nap for a few hours to help you rest."

"Yes please! Can I get two?" I tried to smile. She nodded.

"I'll see you in a few hours." She smiled.

Clyde reclined on the sofa in the room, watching television and dozing off. I sent Trevor a text message. Everything began to move in slow motion after the doctor inserted the epidural and I was able to recline more comfortably.

The next thing I heard was Dr. Alson announce that I had dilated seven centimeters and we'd be ready to push in thirty more minutes. I prepared mentally for labor, as I envisioned the nightmares I had heard of being in labor sometimes twenty plus hours.

She returned and reminded me of my breathing, while walking me through what I could expect and instructions of what to do. After she scrubbed up, we did a couple of preliminary pushes and then she announced the baby was already crowning.

"Are you ready to meet your baby, Olivia? He's ready to meet you! You can do this!" Dr. Alson declared.

It was time. I was going to finally meet my little bean pod, as I referred to him. "I can do this!" I whispered to myself.

She instructed we'd begin pushing again in just a minute, as she stepped away to glove up. In that moment, I felt tremendous pressure in my cervix and could feel my baby sliding down, but I couldn't move.

"I think you need to hurry!" I said anxiously.

The nurse quickly assisted with Dr. Alson's mask, and as she turned to look behind the sheet draped across my lower abdomen, she had a surprised look on her face.

"He's ready now! We've got a strong one. Okay, Olivia, I need one good, deep breath and a push," Dr. Alson coached.

I did just as instructed, as if I was in a military boot camp. I was good at following directions.

"Now, let's do that a few more times. Good breath and another push." Dr. Alson looked pleased, as she nodded in affirmation.

After another push, I felt the pressure release and my baby glide out.

"Meet your little boy!" Dr. Alson held up my baby boy. I was elated. I forgot Clyde was in the delivery room, until the doctor looked back at him and asked if he wanted to cut the cord. She instructed him where.

She held him up. "He's healthy." She placed my baby on my chest. "And this is your mommy." Within seconds, the nurse was showing me how to get him to latch onto my breast, though I always assumed it would be natural. It was painful and required some art form to make certain for a good experience for both of us. *I am happy I took the breast-feeding class.* There was nothing natural about it, at least, not for me. I was not an artist.

"You did great, Olivia! He's perfect and he's beautiful," Dr. Alson whispered as she lowered her head down to us both. I noticed Clyde slowly pacing, stopping to sit on the couch.

"Thank you, Doc! I appreciate you more than you know, and thank you for bringing my baby here safe." Tears welled in my eyes.

"I knew you would do great! How do you feel?" Dr. Alson stroked my tummy.

"I'm in love!" I smiled. The tears began to flow, as I bent my head to kiss my baby's head, as he nursed.

"You deserve all the love you can stand, Olivia. Get some rest, too, while you can." Her eyebrows went up sternly.

I was overwhelmed with elation, love, relief and joy.

"Remember what we talked about. I, or one of the nurses, will be near at all times and the nurse can take him to the nursery if you need to rest." Dr. Alson spoke quietly to me. "I'll be back to check on you and the baby in about an hour."

I nodded. "I will." She said something to the nurse and stepped out.

"Hey, Jordan, it's Mommy. I love you!" I repeated those words over and over, stroking his back, as I stared at him in amazement.

After thirty minutes of breast-feeding, the nurse took my baby bedside to sponge bathe and clean him up, while taking the necessary measurements and administering whatever tests and medicines were required. I watched with admiration, thankful for the blessing of his arrival to this world healthy. I cried tears of joy, almost uncontrollably as I reflected on the last ten months and felt relief emerging to this side full of peace. I knew my steps had been perfectly ordered, in a perfect way along my journey and all my sorrow had turned to joy. I was smiling. Inside and out.

I was enjoying bonding with my son and, even though I had a feeling to tell Clyde what I knew, it was all so surreal and so unfortunate at the same time. As in any break up of a relationship, it is always difficult in some way, but even more with a child and, though I can't articulate words like hurt or anger or even betrayal to what I felt, feelings of a void did exist for me to share my child with someone I not only had no interest in, but sadly, had no respect for. I didn't want to judge Clyde, but I did have to question his motives and his behavior as a parent; motives to me that were concerning at best and which spoke volumes to his character.

I knew the road to conquer those feelings of disdain for Clyde would be a long one, but it was a road I was committed to travel to ensure the emotional stability and wellness of my son because he deserved that.

I think Clyde was in shock or maybe he was resentful, as he stood motionless watching me holding Jordan across my naked chest. I would have liked to believe maybe the birth touched him in some great way and made a move on his heart, but I knew better, as his eyes had the same cold stare I had seen so many times before. If the news itself, hearing the heartbeat or witnessing the image of the baby inside my belly, hadn't caused one ounce of change, then I knew better to think witnessing giving life and life itself would move anything. I couldn't want for Clyde what he didn't want for himself, but for our son's sake,

I would continue to pray and I would take the right fork in the road to move on.

I stayed up all night enjoying my little one sleeping on my chest and relished in just listening to him breathe, staring at every inch of his magnificent creation with complete wonderment. Plans in my head whirled, as I thought of our pending departure and though something told me the battle had just begun with Clyde, I resigned myself to take the high road and do what was right for my child.

Trevor called a few times while I was in the hospital to check on the baby and me, and wondered how I was holding up with the charade of it all. I shared with him the excitement of just having gave birth and being relieved and excited for what was ahead. He was happy this day was here for me and we looked forward to seeing one another soon.

As I held my baby close to me, I whispered a story about God's angel that granted me one wish. I told of how I asked the angel for a sweet bundle of joy to share with, to laugh with and to grow with, and the angel agreed to grant my wish as long as I promised to always take care of that bundle of joy, to never leave him and to always love him with every ounce of my being. I avowed to the angel that I would keep my promise always and forever.

As I lay in the hospital that evening thinking, foresight was already telling me it would make for a simpler life if I never put Clyde on the birth certificate, especially not being married, but I was caught up in the stereotype of being an unwed mother and what others thought of me. At that moment, I decided not to live in regret and to cast my burden on the Highest Power and focus on the bigger picture.

We were nearing the holidays and I had agreed to stay in Chicago through the New Year for Clyde's family to meet Jordan. He planned a visit with his family over Thanksgiving holiday. I opted to visit my family in the springtime, after our move, without Clyde. It also gave me the opportunity to tighten the final bits of my finances and my plan. I was looking forward to getting back to Charlotte and seeing Layla and my old friends and colleagues again. People I could learn and grow from, now in another aspect of life—being a mother.

When I broke the news to Clyde that weekend that our move was finalized and we'd be moving the month after our return from the holiday, we got into a heated argument and he stormed out with his usual dramatic exit, as does someone who portrays the victim.

The next morning at eight a.m., a police officer rang the apartment to inform me of an incident that landed Clyde in jail. Something about being in jail and a phone number to call to check when he'd be released. I was awakened from my sleep and still somewhat groggy, not even realizing it was morning or that Clyde hadn't returned home that night. I did realize it was the first night Jordan and I slept through the night since coming home from the hospital. I didn't call the number.

"What happened to you?" I said, surprised when Clyde walked through the door some forty hours later, with muddied and torn clothes. I paused as I emptied the dishwasher.

He didn't answer, starring me down as he passed me. The stench in the air followed him. He appeared to be in some distress, as he walked with a limp.

"An officer came by and said you were arrested. He didn't tell me much." My voice trailed as he walked away.

"I have no idea what happened, but some police officers beat me up and I blacked out," he scowled, balling his fist and examining its mobility. He slammed the door to the bathroom. I hoped that meant he was taking a long shower. His vague admittance that something was inappropriate said enough.

I made a few phone calls to Trevor to look into the matter.

I made the safe and probably correct assumption that whatever happened, large quantities of alcohol were consumed since Clyde didn't know what happened. Unfortunately, given his vague explanation of what happened and portraying himself as the victim, again, Clyde would continue to live in his wretchedness. I let him think I believed him and even pitied him for what happened, but the truth was I just didn't care; I did pity him, but not for the reasons he believed. I just wanted to keep peace until I left.

It was going to be a long few days with Clyde around the apartment.

Trevor helped doing legal research regarding the state laws in Chicago and having a child out of wedlock. He also called in a few favors and connected me with a couple of attorneys to consult with to know my rights. Chicago was one of the more liberal states that would afford me a percentage off the top, in addition to expenses for child support, and since I didn't have a regular income, expenses would be one hundred percent Clyde's responsibility. Counsel also advised that given what happened with Clyde and the altercation with the police, he would be waiting for a court date, which would not be for four to six months and no court would make a single mother stay in the same state with a father with an arrest.

In the coming days, Clyde stayed home being in some physical distress since Chicago PD supposedly kicked the crap out of him. He was behaving irrationally, locking himself and the baby in the bedroom when it was the baby's feeding time, threatening that if Jordan didn't take the bottle, he wouldn't eat. I lost it when I heard Jordan's crying escalate.

"You give me my baby!" I screamed, as I pounded on the door.

"Not until he eats! You always get to feed him and he's going to eat from me this time," Clyde scoffed.

"Either you open this door or I'll call the police. They'd love to take you down again and finish what they started!" I began pacing from the hall to the living area. Clyde opened the door and stormed down the hallway.

"Don't push me! I am not responsible for what I do to you!" he yelled. The baby's cries turned to shrieks.

"You either bring me my child or I will call the police and tell them that you hit me!" I burst out, holding my cell phone in the air.

"You can't threaten me!" He took a leap, striking my hand, which hit the radiator.

My phone hit the floor and shattered. I recoiled my wrist close to my body in pain, noticing it immediately began to bruise. The shrill of my baby crying stiffened my body and I quickly ran to the bedroom. I was surprised to find Jordan turned on his side. It had only been five weeks, but my nerves were tense to appreciate this moment.

Clyde yelled something and stormed out.

I was silent and confused, though he had no idea that I did my homework and knew exactly my rights. He would not intimidate me anymore. I was going to make better choices.

⤿

Our departure for Tucson was set for the Thanksgiving holiday, the next week, though I didn't know how I was going to last seven days in a city I knew nothing of, knew no one and had nowhere to go, let alone survive his family.

I was uneasy since meeting his mother when she visited Chicago, leaving me with more disturbing concerns about the pedigree that stood out so blaringly. Besides finding it peculiar that a grown man referred to his mother by her first name and had for years, Clyde went out of his way to continually impress and satisfy her, as she hopelessly believed what she wanted about her son because anything more would make her accountable, lending to the feelings of entitlement he, not surprisingly, adopted. Or, perhaps she knew exactly the offspring she raised and the fruit didn't fall far from the tree, as she silently supported him, hiding behind the guise of not wanting to get involved. The irony of such an appearing close relation was Clyde's twisted and blatant retaliation of mistreatment and hatred toward women, making it all the more troubling.

I met Lauren, Clyde's cousin in-law, the day after Thanksgiving. Lauren appeared to be in her mid-forties. She was attractive and wore a natural, short Afro and her body was thick and fit. She was a day trader looking for a transfer from California, where she currently lived, with her company to the Tucson area, to be closer to family. She was visiting her family for the holidays and brought the kids by to visit, Clyde's mother, who I came to understand also raised her nephew from a deceased sibling as her own and has been a grandma to his and now Lauren's children. She had four-year-old twins.

"Girl, you look tired," she said when we had a moment to be alone and the others had scattered inside playing with their new toys.

"I've been up most of the night because Jordan caught an ear infection and I've been awake all night. He's sleeping now, thank goodness." I helplessly shook my head.

"I swear it must be something in the water out here!" Lauren rolled her eyes back at the house, stepping outside for more privacy. The home sat on a corner somewhat distant to the other homes in the neighborhood and backed up into a park. There was not much activity on the street, much like the rest of the neighborhood.

"You think?" I couldn't help but chuckle.

"Or someone, but I'm thankful it's not my issue," Lauren said sadly. We both looked around. The desolateness was eerie.

"There's a common denominator here for sure."

"Yes, there's a common denominator and don't be fooled by Clyde always trying to be the mediator." She paused. "I've lived it for four years, but we're divorced now. I visit because this is who my children know as their family and they deserve to know them. I didn't expect any help, but I did expect people to stand behind what is right and wrong. That's all." Her eyes began to water. "I just wanted it to stop."

"I am so sorry!" I paused at a loss for words. I looked up and down the street. It was barren, except for cars parked in the driveways. My mind couldn't grasp what I was hearing. "I wish I would have met you earlier."

"I do, too. Just take the high road as far as they are all concerned and do right by your child. Love and protect him."

"We're moving back to Charlotte a few weeks after we get back."

"I wish I would have left sooner, but I stayed for the children." She looked reflective. "Children are smart and even when you think you are doing a good thing by staying; their innocent souls get so caught up in all the emotion and get so confused. They are so precious." I felt her stare pierce through my soul. She saw my hurt. We were the same.

"I don't know how you did it as long as you did, but the most important thing is, there is so much to look forward to." I was hopeful, looking out at the park and the wide-open space. I remembered the Greenway. She called to the kids. Sadness began to well up inside me, although I wasn't sure where it came from. Maybe that's how you feel when you feel someone's hurt. You feel helpless.

"We're smart women." Lauren stood in front of me, putting her hands on my shoulders. "Please, and I mean this sincerely, take care of yourself for that baby of yours. He needs you well!" The kids came rushing outside full of excitement with there new toys in hand. Suddenly, the very heavy air was lighter with the squeals of joy.

"I most certainly will. I'm so glad I got a chance to talk to you. Promise me you'll do the same."

Clyde and his mother slowly followed the kids outside, while they chatted and laughed.

"I better go." I leaned to give Lauren a hug, sensing her anxiety to leave. She exchanged some words with the family.

Lauren put the kids in their car seats and helped them with their seatbelts. She paused. "It's a parent's job to raise conscientious and accountable children that ultimately assimilate into a society with morals and values or they both shall reap the consequences. When one bad egg in the offspring exists, you chalk it up to a rebellious nature, but more than one, you have to take a hard look in the mirror and look for a common denominator. Parenting is not easy and no one is perfect. I better run." Something told me I needed to heed that advice myself.

She waved a distant goodbye to everyone. The kids did also. I stood watching, as she backed up and drove off. I didn't know much of her situation other than the bits and pieces I'd overheard. I never asked any questions.

I was thankful to my parents for raising me with integrity and accountability and, although my siblings and I were far from perfect, they raised independent and considerate human beings.

The seven days seemed like twenty, but I was just glad it wasn't more. There were only two days left to go.

Interlude

SERENITY is not about the fight; it's knowing when not to.

If we embrace our reality, we can have the COURAGE to live the possibilities.

Sometimes in life we have to make a new path, the WISDOM is in knowing which path to take.

Seven
HINDSIGHT

⊶

THE CHARADE WAS OVER. I WAS free and was regaining my dignity, self-respect and grace where it was once lost.

Things started coming to light, literally, from the moment I arrived and shared Clyde's space, and all the lies caught up to one another when I was seven-and-a-half months pregnant, less than four weeks to the day I moved to Chicago. It had been God's favor to move us back to Charlotte with a better plan than I could've planned myself. It had been a year, almost to the day, that I met Clyde, three months of dating, two cities, a pregnancy, Jordan was born and going full circle moving back to Charlotte. I couldn't think of a more appropriate way to start a new year of being free to make a fresh start. Something about a new year that always brought so much promise.

We'd been back in Charlotte for a few months and I was enjoying every minute of our days. Still on maternity leave, I would have given anything to stay off as long as I could with Jordan to soak up his every move and squeals of delight. Jordan was a healthy, happy baby and we were finding our way in our new life.

Clyde had visited Charlotte once to see Jordan and I allowed him to stay at my home, taking the doctor's advice with the baby. One evening, Clyde demanded to use my car.

"I just need to get out for a little while," he pleaded. You would have thought he was on his last drop of water.

"I'm sorry, but I can't be stranded without a car with a baby in case of an emergency."

"You just want me to stay home with you so you can control me!" He started pacing the living room.

"Clyde, may I remind you that I left Chicago! It should have been clear to you then that I'm not interested in controlling you. And, I know better!" My heart began to beat faster, as I walked to the door of Jordan's room to peek in on him. He was sleeping. I remained calm, standing beside the kitchen counter that housed the panic button directly connected to the police station that was literally my backyard. One of the reasons I decided to move here.

"You stole my child and you abandoned me." He sounded desperate.

"I can't steal something that belongs to me, and I didn't abandon you if that was the plan from the beginning. This is my house and you will not raise your voice in my house. I invited you to stay at our home to spend time with your son, but I'd like you to leave now." I spoke calmly. "We can arrange for you to visit with Jordan in the daytime if you are still in the city." My lack of interest seemed to antagonize him more, as he stormed around gathering his things. He slammed the door on the way out.

I wasn't expecting that Clyde would change, but I prayed he'd step up for his child and be a responsible father. I also recognized I couldn't want for someone what they didn't want for themselves. In the meantime, I definitely didn't want my child to have to be subject to the hurt and inconsistency of a sometime father until he decided what he wanted. Intention spoke volumes, and Clyde's lack thereof would make itself apparent sooner than later.

I kept busy caring for a six-month-old round the clock, and although I was enjoying every minute with my little one, the reality was I couldn't stay home indefinitely. I was thankful for my company supporting me throughout this entire ordeal, relocating me to Chicago and now back again to Charlotte, all in a year. I was happy to be working with Layla again. I could use her strength and insight since becoming a mom. And, I looked forward to getting together with Candace and Abigail, and Aunt Ernestine especially.

My career had always been important to me and I had done well with this third—and longest running—career path. It had afforded me a more than comfortable life with many experiences, both professionally and personally, which helped shape the person I had become. I had saved some sizeable savings over the years, with the market being on my side, but now with resources being depleted, it was time to replenish the stash. This time around, I'd have more flexibility to work from home and got a promotion to Senior Vice President of Advertising. I was worried the new position would be more challenging and stressful now being a mom. I was returning to work in two weeks.

For what seemed to be on hold for an eternity, I was just happy to snip the last string that tied me to Clyde to cancel the insurance policy I had purchased, against my better judgment, after Jordan was born. I took the day off to manage some personal matters, catch a workout and pick Jordan up early at the daycare.

"Ms. Thompson, are you still there?" I was pacing my living room floor, stopping to look outside the window at the clear sky.

"Yes," I said anxiously.

"Because you are not the owner of that policy, you are not authorized to cancel the policy. You are the insured, but the insured is not authorized to make any changes. Only the owner can make changes," she offered.

I felt a dull knot forming in my stomach, with what I was hearing. Actually, it was more like stabbing and it had been there for the past year since meeting Clyde.

"Can you tell me who the owner is? And what is your name, so I can just make a record of who I spoke with?"

"Yes. My name is Penny Sullivan. It looks like your fiancé, Mr. Clyde Walters, is the owner."

I choked on the water I was sipping, spitting it all over the phone receiver. *Fiancé,* I thought. *Surely, she made a mistake.* "Fiancé?" I vocalized my thoughts. "We're not engaged, never were, and never will be for that matter! There must be some mistake." *I wish I had a latte to calm my nerves.* "We each got policies after our son was born and we were each supposed to be the respective owners of our policies. Are you sure the information you have is correct? Can you check again?" I began pacing again, as I felt my blood pressure rising. Ironically, the sky now seemed grey. I must have projected how I was feeling.

"Yes, that's what it says and that's why I put you on hold because I wanted to go over it with another colleague to make sure." Ms. Sullivan sounded like a sensible young lady and like she knew what she was reading.

"Clyde's friend from college, Anthony Perkins, works at your company and he sold them to us. He must have made a mistake," I pleaded, although quickly realizing the contrary. *It was no mistake,* I thought.

"I see the address is in Chicago, but I don't show that Mr. Perkins is licensed in Illinois in my employee directory. Who did you meet with?"

"No one." I was infuriated to think the person who swore to God was actually a compulsive liar and had charmed the common sense right out of me. It was all coming back to me, as I remembered Clyde's persistence in wanting to secure a policy, though not willing to consider any other options other than the company where his friend worked.

"Did anyone come to your home and do a physical?" Penny asked, trying to find some explanation.

"Yes, she said she was a nurse. I forgot her name, but I am sure it's on the file."

"Oh, yes I see. Did you sign some paperwork?" She sounded like she was reading from a script. I felt like I was the one reading from a script. A horror movie script.

"Yes, a beneficiary designation form."

"Was that all? Did you fill out an application?"

"No. I did inquire about the application with the nurse when she came to do the physical, but she told me the agent would provide it. I never received anything and I never met with anyone else."

"I'm showing Clyde Walters as the beneficiary. Did you make Mr. Walters the beneficiary?"

"Absolutely not! He must have changed the beneficiaries. Unbelievable, but I can't say I'm surprised!" The movie script was now very real to me.

"We'll need to investigate further and, given the dollar amount of this policy, we wouldn't pay out under these circumstances without an investigation anyhow. I'm not sure how or why it was set up this way and I don't see where it was ever verified. For that dollar amount, we typically get a notarized statement from the insured aware that the policy exists and a sign off from upper management. I know I wouldn't want someone having a policy on me, especially if I didn't know about it. That's just scary!" She sounded as though she understood, as she offered some explanation. She was not reading from a script anymore and her voice switched to concern. "Thanks for bringing this to our attention, Ms. Thompson, and I am so sorry this is happening to you. We will be in contact very soon. Is there anything else I can do for you today?"

"Please, just do whatever you can, as soon as you can, to get this cancelled. And, keep me posted with what you find out. Thank you, Ms. Sullivan."

"Yes, ma'am. We will be in touch very soon."

I hung up the phone and looked at the time, realizing I needed to head out to meet Walter for one of our regular workouts before picking Jordan up at daycare. Still in shock as I got in my car, I called my attorney. She was in depositions and my mind instantly jumped at the opportunity to kick into overtime. I was literally driving in slow motion, as my mind wandered.

All I could think was I was set up, knowing my intuition never failed me, but rather that I had failed to listen. I wasn't a fan of mixing personal matters with business, especially finances with friends or family, but I gave in to yet another one of Clyde's lies. In this case, a story about trying to help his depressed friend since he was short on money. At the time, I concluded his friend must have really needed the commission, which I learned amounted to a paltry five hundred dollars, which made me wonder if Clyde genuinely wanted to help his friend, why he wouldn't have just given him the money. The more I learned, the more I didn't want to know, as I replayed the entire incident in my mind and should've trusted my gnawing instinct as everything started to make sense now in retrospect.

At the very least, it didn't make sense to me being that Clyde was a University of Pennsylvania Medical grad and made some of the dumbest money management decisions I ever came across, or maybe it made perfect sense for liars that live without consequence when they try to deceive. What was making sense was that Clyde and his crew would sell their souls and their principles for a dollar, and they were master manipulators of fraud. I turned into the gym parking lot, not quite conscious of the past twelve minutes driving there. The sad reality was that the father of my child was able to secure the life insurance policy and his friend was able to facilitate it all for a measly five hundred dollars. Unfortunately, even sadder for both of them to think I would not figure it out or worse, that I would not quash these wrongdoings. I did know forgery didn't have a statute of limitations and there was something called a public record.

Glancing around, I didn't notice Walter's car and impatiently decided to dial Anthony. Instantly realizing Clyde probably wanted to exchange the obligatory 'in case of emergency' contacts after the baby was born, knowing he was securing a life insurance policy on my life. My faith stood bigger than my fear, knowing I had survived a fatal attraction twenty years earlier and a car wreck that left me learning to walk again for a reason. Today was that reason.

"This is Anthony." I heard his voice for the first time, which now seemed especially weird knowing I was talking to the person that fraudulently facilitated and executed a life insurance policy on my life. His voice was deep, with a heavy southern twang. It had just occurred to me that I knew nothing about this person. I took a hard swallow to stop myself from gagging.

"Anthony, this is Olivia, your friend Clyde's ex. I just found out the life insurance policy you sold me is in Clyde's name. What is going on?" Realizing after saying those words how pointless it was, since there must have been some serious history between these two if they were willing to both risk everything. I enviously watched an energetic gym regular grab his bag from his car trunk to head into the gym, seemingly without a care in the world.

"What do you mean 'ex'? When did that happen?" By my silence, he could tell I wasn't interested in small talk. He continued. "Um…the policy was set up that way," Anthony replied, as though that was the intent. Clearly.

"Anthony, I live in Charlotte now. I didn't fill out an application and I am not sure how you were able to execute this. Since you were my supposed agent, you need to resolve this and I need you to call Clyde and have him cancel the policy! He's conveniently not taking my calls."

"Okay. I'll give him a call and call you back." From his tone, I could hear I had been played the fool. I recognized the same dismissive response I had gotten so often from Clyde in the past when he had been caught with his pants down, in wonderment of my knowledge, a sick sense of entitlement and no wrongdoing. "But can I ask you not to cancel until December, when my commission posts?" I was speechless. These goons were incurable and I trusted they would reap what they so deceitfully had sown. I hung up. I guess it did come down to five hundred dollars. Were times really that hard, or was it the game of deceit that these characters lusted after?

Walter drove up and parked in the parking spot next to mine. I grew madder with unbelief this was happening, feeling violated and foolish at the same time.

I wanted to give Clyde's friend a chance to rectify this situation or else I'd pursue filing a complaint with his company and the insurance commissioner for insurance fraud, misrepresentation, not being licensed in the state of doing business and falsifying records. I knew enough about insurance to know that the insurance industry takes licensing very serious, not to mention the code of ethics and the regulatory directives. Whatever it was, I was going after it, even if it meant I would have to pursue criminal charges.

Walter proceeded to get out of his car.

"You won't believe the latest!" I got out of my car, slamming the door. His shoulders looked broader than I remembered, or maybe it was the t-shirt he wore that made them protrude more.

"What now?" We greeted each other with our usual hug.

"Oh, just that my baby's dad and his friend ran a game on me and took out a million-dollar policy on my life."

"Are you serious? Damn! How do you even do that?"

"As a heart attack!" We walked inside the gym and checked in at the front desk. The young lady gave Walter the biggest smile I think I'd ever witnessed across her face. Walter was indeed ruggedly handsome with a boyish magnetic smile that could knock the pants right off of you, completely unaware. His salt goatee accentuated his chocolate skin and chiseled jawbone.

"This guy is certifiable!" We walked towards the free weight area. I felt like throwing some weights to release my frustration. The crowd was thin before the after work rush hour.

"Who does this stuff Walter and what did I do wrong?"

"Your baby daddy, that's who." Walter laughed, looking over my shoulder, nodding to someone familiar. I missed the comfort of his laugh. "Don't try to reason with insanity. Girl, you didn't do anything wrong. You were just being you. That's enough to make anyone crazy!" Walter gave me one of those smiles.

"How did I miss this? I mean, he seemed at least a little put together, being a University of Pennsylvania doctor, although I don't even know that to be true."

"He lied about that, too?"

"I'm just saying, I've never seen a diploma and I've never gone to his office or the hospital," I said sarcastically.

It was chest-and-back day and Walter always pushed me beyond my limits on days like this, purposefully redirecting my focus and energy, or maybe it was his own intensity that made me push myself. I craved the energy and focus of working out with someone that pushed me, not to mention the comfort of knowing Walter.

"Well, I do know this about you; you don't fall for degrees or dollars, but for some guys it's about the conquest and control for them. I'm pretty sure liars and crazy people go to University of Pennsylvania too, you know." Walter chuckled, stacking the weights on the chest press for his set. I just watched, noticing his biceps bulge. "Once you figured him out and didn't play by his rules, his ego couldn't take it." He exhaled. "So now he's got to traumatize and intimidate you, to feel like he's won. Rest in the fact that it's a matter of numbers for him and he'll move on to his next victim. He'll eventually meet his match. People like him always do." I noticed a couple in the corner on the squat press exchanging a laugh, as the man casually stroked the lady's thigh for her to focus her strength.

"Remember when I told you I was just hanging out and he didn't have any conversation and that it would play itself out?" Walter was nodding. "Well, I broke it off with him the next week when I found out he cheated and three weeks later I found out I was pregnant!" I stood over Walter and watched him position himself down on the bench, his eyes focused on the bar below me. He took a deep and slow breath.

"I do remember that. I guess it did play itself out. I still can't believe a guy would step out on you. I could never get enough and when I left you, I couldn't wait to see you again." I watched his barrel chest rise and fall as he pushed through each repetition. "Girl, I just thought the sex must have been mind blowing and he turned you out because I just knew there had to be something." He grew animated as he returned the bar to the machine. "Just keep doing what's best for your son. How's he doing by the way? You guys need to come hang out at the pool again and we'll barbeque."

"He's great! I really appreciate you being so kind and helpful to us. And, on another note, I can only say that the sex was uneventful." I glared at him.

"Girlfriend, just keep looking ahead and don't look back...
or go back, or I'll slap you myself!" He nudged my shoulder, as
he stood. "I'm joking, but for real, I've always thought and do
think you are an amazing woman, and if this man or any man
can't see that, they don't deserve you! It's that simple." He was
removing the weights for my much lighter set.

"Walter, you've always been my biggest supporter. Please
know I will always love you for that no matter where our lives
take us, and I always want everything for you that you want.
I know I'm in my season of harvest and better days are ahead
for my little guy and me. Faith is my beacon!" I looked around
the gym before laying down, avoiding further discussion to
offset the emotion that was growing inside me. Some people
were focused, seemingly lost in thought while others exchanged
dialogue and laughs.

"So what are you going to do about the policy, Olivia?"
Walter's voice switched to concern. "Do I need to call in a favor
to some of my boys in Chicago?"

"Take a number. I have a few friends that want to call in a
favor. Guess it's good to know people, but my God is bigger than
all of this." I took a deep breath, as I lifted the bar off the clips.

"Seriously, Olivia. You're a good person and when I hear
about guys trying to intimidate you...I get mad! He needs a little
rattling himself."

Just then, I heard my phone ringing in my gym bag. I returned
the bar after my set.

It was Anthony calling me back.

"Speaking of, this is his friend. I'm going to step in the changing room and take the call. I'm curious to hear what explanation he gives."

"Me too! Do what you gotta do. I'm going to get another set."

"Hello?" I answered, walking toward the ladies changing room.

"Hey, Olivia, this is Anthony. I spoke to Clyde and, in fact, we've been talking all day and he said, um…he's not going to cancel the policy." He hesitated.

I realized I was dealing with nothing more than a few disguised thugs that tried to run a scandal on me, and could only assume people don't keep running the same game unless someone has taken the bait or they're just addicted to deceit and manipulation. I think it was a solid combination of both and the latter made me sick to consider. My jaw protruded, as I clenched my teeth to refrain from cursing. I began pacing.

"Anthony, I've never met you, but I learned you weren't licensed in Chicago to sell me the policy. I want to be clear of my intention and where I'm coming from and give you the opportunity to correct your convenient mistake, but you leave me no choice but to pursue legal action with your company and the insurance commissioner. " I spoke tersely, looking at myself standing square in front of a floor length mirror, my hand on my narrow hips, noticing I had lost considerable weight with the stress.

"Um, yes, I am not licensed in the state of Chicago, so I sent the paperwork through my colleague in our Chicago office."

Anthony hesitated again. *These types are quick on their feet with the lies they tell,* I thought.

"Oh, yes, another person I didn't meet who sold me the counterfeit policy. I didn't even fill out an application!" My eyes grew sullen, staring in the mirror. I noticed the dark circles under my eyes.

There was an awkward extended pause.

"I can ask him again, but he's in anger management counseling tonight." He tried to offer some consolation sounding hopeless himself.

"That's hilarious and pathetic, but thanks. I would think you would do anything to ensure this policy gets cancelled if it means your livelihood," I suggested. I didn't know what Clyde had told him with his twisted perception, but I was determined not to let these two hustlers maneuver me anymore. I was still pacing back and forth, as a few more people walked into the change area. I glanced at the clock, noting it would be time to leave soon to pick up Jordan, wanting to get a few more sets in.

"Okay, thanks." I hung up in disbelief at the absurdity. Given it was Friday, anger management for Clyde probably meant sitting up in a bar drinking, while he complained and preyed on another victim, while acting like one.

Taking a moment to gather my thoughts, I shook my head and joined Walter.

"Fill me in?" Walter nudged me.

"Clyde is not going to cancel it and get this…he's going to anger management counseling tonight."

"What the... The classes clearly aren't working for him if he schemed to get a life insurance policy in the first place. Oh, how I'd love to knock some sense into him." I could hear it in Walter's voice that he meant that. Walter was built like a machine and could take most. Favors would not be necessary. This was not my battle.

"I told you it's the world according to Clyde and everyone else has the problem. He'll get his!" I sat on the incline press, as I extended my neck, and took a few deep breaths to get focused.

"You know, I tried to give the guy some credit, thinking you were being your hard self, but he's more serious than I thought. It angers me when I hear about sorry guys because they give good guys like me a bad name! They're the first to say they can't find a good woman, but when they find one, they don't know how to treat them and then when the woman has had enough and cuts them off, they can't handle it. They act like the victim and try to justify their own wrongdoings. He's angry with someone. Either his parents or some girl that played him in college or some guy that knocked him upside his head. He needs to do himself a favor, and get over himself real quick and get over you because you and the rest of the world, including his son, are living life. He'll still be doing this same mess years from now. Someone will have him between a rock and a hard place, literally and figuratively, before it's all said and done. And, he'll have no one to thank, but himself because what goes around comes around. Seriously though, he really does need counseling for whatever has him conflicted, but girlfriend, it's not you! These are all his issues!" Walter had a disgusted look on his face.

"This is what they call people living with a sense of entitlement without a purpose. They prey upon others to inflict their hurt." I sighed. "But I don't want to talk about his misery anymore. He'd want nothing more. I just want to finish my workout, go pick up Jordan, and give him a great big hug. I have my own battles of which I have the ability to change. As much as Clyde wants me to believe I was the problem, I know I'm not and I know he had these issues long before I came on the scene. I just brought them to the surface. And, he had the nerve to say I tried to trap him and I even gave him back every piece of jewelry he ever gave me."

"Darn! You gave it back? You're better than me! Darn, I wish some of my exes would give theirs back." He chuckled. "You need to focus on this last set. Let's get it." I pushed through it.

"I don't have any use for them!" I chuckled, replacing the bar on the stand.

"I'm just glad you're back and I am glad you are not with him. Sometimes in life, we lose ourselves, but that is when you find yourself. It's not about the other person anyway. In this case, you did it for your son and it was completely selfless and you got nothing from doing it, then or now, and you did the best you could do with the information you had at the time. Focus on the positive and the experience and throw all the other nonsense out!" Walter affirmed.

"I would have preferred to experience Bali or Pilates?" I chuckled. "I get it! You are so right!" I noticed that same couple from the squat press wrapping up their session, as the young lady reached up to give the considerably taller man a hug. Her body language indicated it was a hug of friendly appreciation. The same I felt for Walter.

"You said the distance would play itself out on its own and that's why I didn't think too much on it, but this dude is acting like a straight up punk!" We finished up another set and moved to another weight machine, as we motored through the end of our routine.

"Not you, too? A lot of people have told me that." I shook my head in defeat.

"I mean you break up with someone, you move on. Life goes on. What's all the drama about? You're only guilty of giving someone a chance that didn't deserve one. You can never be wrong for that. That means you're human. You gave a dude the benefit of the doubt and wanted to see the good in him, but he just wasn't and you got out. You went, you saw and you left." Walter desperately sounded supportive.

"And I just want him to leave me alone."

"He's acting this way because you are the one that left him and you turned his world upside down. He knows he's to blame for the relationship's demise and there's no harder guilt for a man than his own recognizance, but it's easier to put the guilt trip on you, although the only trip this guy should be on is his own."

"I'm just glad I left. What goes around will come around!" I pushed through my final rep on the decline bench.

"Indeed it will! Remember I'm speaking from experience and I know who you are." Walter looked at me endearingly.

"Truthfully, most men won't know how to handle you because you're real and you don't do much drama, especially anyone else's!" Walter gave me another one of those smiles.

"Darn, you make me sound cold?" I teased.

"No, you're real. You broke my heart, but you helped me heal, too, and that I'm forever thankful for. That's good stuff! Don't change a thing because of this fool."

"I hear you." I needed that.

"Do you feel me? I'm serious. Your challenge is finding a man up to the challenge and bringing exactly what you give on all levels. Mentally, emotionally and physically." Walter was shaking his head for confirmation.

"I feel you!" I stood, staring around. The gym was more barren than the usual weekday since it was Friday. My mind wandered to thoughts of many a day and night Walter and I just lounged, talking about anything or nothing and feeling completely at ease with either. He always made me feel stronger like I could take on the world.

Walter and I gathered our things and exited the gym. We parted with a hug; a hug of appreciation, thankfulness and a love for one another that ran deep. Walter embraced longer than usual and, as our bodies separated, he reached to kiss my forehead. Getting in my car, I was thankful to have friends like Walter that cared, even with all the changes my life was going through.

I couldn't help but smile, knowing God had called me above all I experienced to be here; to carry Jordan for almost ten of the most blessed months of my life, to labor him gently and safely into this world and to have my name forever changed to "Mom." This was the favor that was on my life, I was still standing, and I was thankful for all my supportive friends that helped me to be here.

As I drove to pick up Jordan, I noticed the trees that lined the streets hover with enormous grace, as I was swallowed with thoughts of my state of affairs. I wasn't sure if continuing to work under such stress was the best choice, but I had just recently returned from maternity leave and I wasn't independently wealthy. Not to mention, health insurance and, most importantly, a much needed distraction in an effort to gain Olivia back—one piece at a time—even if it meant longer hours around the clock and more coffee to balance it all.

Peeking into Jordan's class, I was more delighted than the day he was born when I saw his eyes see mine. Unbeknownst to him, he held the power to make everything well again. To whom much is given much is indeed required, and there was nothing I wouldn't do for all that I was given. All was better in my world, as he spread his little arms and hands up for me to pick him up. I gave him the biggest hug and twirled him around, as I buried my tears in his shoulder. I was his enormous tree and felt overwhelmingly blessed and thankful at that moment, and just wanted to make sure the rest of his day was full of tickles and laughs until bedtime, every day better than the last.

Eight
LOST

I REFUSED VISITATION SINCE FINDING OUT Clyde had taken a million-dollar life insurance policy on my life and refused to cancel it, not knowing what he was capable of and whether he wanted to cause harm to me, intimidate me or cause harm to the baby; none of which were healthy for me or the child. Everything considered, he didn't have anything and by that same token, he didn't have anything to lose. Everything had been for his own personal gain and driven out of fear. He always told me that money gave people options, which was a contradiction the way he spent it, and the irony to that, left him with none.

I proceeded with the legal action. There were extensive document production notices and Interrogatory questions after questions after questions, pending our initial court date. Clyde was clearly a lover scorned, as evidenced by most of his questions that seemingly had nothing to do with my parenting ability and everything to do with my past relationships, which only revealed more clearly his bitterness toward the demise of the relationship. Sadly, as I learned, questions that delved into a person's past prior to the child being born had little to no bearing on a person's ability to parent, but even sadder, had no influence on the effects of the best interest of the child. Our same queries about his past and present relationships were an attempt to expose and determine his continuing lack of good judgment and poor choices with his behaviors, which I thought could indeed impact one's ability to parent, including the people the child is exposed to, with regard to their safety. Sadly, it didn't and clearly just my opinion, which consequently meant nothing.

As disturbing as that is to know, I also learned, short of molesting a child, parents in many states are entitled to visitation, as long as they conceived the child. Even being an alcoholic or an abuser has only limited restrictions and it's the other parties' responsibility to prove the offender is somehow 'unfit' or their judgment is masked where the safety and best interest of a their child is concerned, and that is of course, if and how the state defines the best interest of the child. I was learning more than enough to make my head spin, which most nights it did, when it wasn't just exhausted from everything else I was doing and dealing with.

One afternoon, at a coffee house in the area, I met my attorney to exchange and review the voluminous information. I arrived early to sort through my papers, watching in a daze the patrons that seemingly had not a care in the world other than which seasonal, flavored concoction to order. Their faces wore a smile of instantaneous pleasure as they ordered their very trendy and expensive coffee.

"Olivia, I just have to ask you a question." My attorney looked up from the papers and pictures of Clyde I had given her. "What in the world did you ever see in this guy?" She removed her reading glasses. "You are so beautiful and sharp and I can tell you have a good head on your shoulders."

I shook my head. I felt defeat stare me in the face.

"And for the record, it's just a picture, but men don't really pose for pictures." Debra changed the subject pointing out Clyde's body position in the picture. "Women pose. Men just have their pictures taken and if you catch them smiling, then the cameraman got lucky, but they usually don't smile. I'm just saying." Debra sounded consolatory, with a side of reprimand like a mother that just caught their child lying.

"So I am learning." I felt ashamed when I said that. There was something very official with retaining legal help for your own bad choices. Not to mention the expense.

Debra's gaze followed a patron, as he entered the café and proceeded to the counter to order. She turned back to face me. "What you've told me about him and some of the behaviors now makes more sense. He's definitely angry and carrying on as such."

"I know. I beat myself up pretty good as it is."

"Give yourself more credit. You are smarter than just having fallen for anything and I am sure he pulled out the red carpet." Debra's tone was serious.

"I just wanted to do what was right and what my conscious allowed me to live with," I said, quietly looking around, noticing there were only three other people in the café now.

"You might want to consider talking to a counselor, you know, just to be able to get it all out because this is enough to drive someone crazy, I know and from what I am learning about you, you are smarter than this and God is bigger."

"Yes, He is!" I confirmed smiling. "I think I should," I whispered.

"Good girl! That's all you can do." Debra nodded her head, distracted as she wrote a few words on sticky notes on papers separated in groups by paper clips. She was methodical and organized. Much like myself. I was relieved to have retained her going up in a system I knew nothing of and now feared from what I was learning.

So many thoughts raced through my mind, as I waited for the therapist to wrap up with her prior client. I preferred to refer to us as 'clients' in need of support rather than 'patients', which possibly meant we were in some way broken, quite possibly irreparably. Initially, I was skeptical about counseling, as I had always considered it a lack of strength or mental facility, but only until I recognized my weakness and need for help did I consider opening myself to it. I welcomed the counsel to gain strength, in order to cope and be all I could be for my child, while being all I was created to be. I was realizing that had gotten lost somewhere.

The waiting area was decorated in a minimalist style of décor, with welcoming earth tone colors, oversized pillows and soft lighting that soothed. The artwork was gracefully appointed, though minimal, displaying abstract images of yoga poses glancing outward toward views of oceans and gardens as the haze grew in the distance. It was the appropriate conscious message of harmony and clarity close to your being with ambiguity and obscurity on the periphery.

"Hi! I'm Clara Grady. Please, call me Clara. It's nice to meet you. Who did you say referred you?" A tall lady greeted me in the waiting area, gesturing her hand for me to follow her back to her office. She exuded a confidence and peacefulness with her graceful walk. She wore an elegantly cropped, wavy hairstyle that revealed her natural beauty and symmetrical, delicate facial features.

"Actually, it was both my internal medicine doctor and my attorney who both suggested I talk to someone for stress. I don't feel crazy, but I know I should talk to someone before I explode." I smiled as I sat down.

Her office was decorated in the same style as the waiting area. Peaceful and warm. There were two high back elegant chairs in a brighter hue of orange that bordered the floor-to-ceiling corner windows overlooking an outside courtyard.

"I am sure you are not crazy and many people talk to a counselor and they're not crazy," she defended, as she spoke firmly.

"I'm sorry. I shouldn't have said that. I just had always thought people who needed counselors were a little off, but that of course was until I found myself in my situation needing one, so maybe I should have said, I want to remain sane."

"Sometimes I even think I'm crazy, so I understand," Ms. Clara said aloofly, as she settled in to her chair. "Well…you can surely talk to me about anything and I usually like to take the initial visit just exploring the reasons why you think you may be going crazy." She paused dramatically. "There's that word again. I can suggest ways to help you manage the areas you may need help with and a lot does depend on what you want to get out of the sessions. Sometimes, that's as easy as just talking. I am not here to judge you, but I would like to help you and sometimes we'll explore areas you may not be comfortable with." She looked to me for some affirmation or acknowledgment, as she sat straight up on the edge of her chair, with her hands on her lap. The irony was I felt uncomfortable and comfortable at the same time.

I nodded my head. "Then I think I'm in the right place!" I affirmed, sitting back in my chair. *I am strong.*

"Ok, well, we can start by exploring what you believe is making you feel stressed and why you decided to come see me?"

"Quite simply, I think my son's father is a compulsive liar and he has a very inflated image of himself, and I need to learn how to manage since I have a lifetime in front of me to parent with him and I don't want to be obsessed with the fact that I got involved with someone like him. I want to move forward." I was direct. Something felt lighter inside me. *I could do this,* I thought.

"If it makes you feel better, I hear similar stories and the best thing for you to do would be to consider one thing at a time and we can start with what you noticed when you met, and perhaps ignored, and work backwards, knowing what you know now and fill in the blanks. So many times, the signs are all there, but we fail to listen." She sounded consoling.

"Guilty!" I chuckled nervously.

Ms. Clara settled in her chair crossing her legs. "I haven't heard your story yet, but I'd like to help you accept that sometimes things happen and we may even have to be accountable because we've attracted it and we need to recognize what we are putting out there and change that."

"Apparently, I am hard headed, blind or both and I need a sign in the sky telling me what to do." I paused. "But then I guess life would be easy and we would never learn," I said reflectively, looking out the window. I wanted to stop my mind from racing with reasons, explanations and excuses.

"And sometimes it's simply to prepare you for things to come. It may just be that your story can help someone else going through something."

"I know I need to change the way I think of my son's father, for my son, because I don't want to harbor resentment and block my blessings either."

"That's a very healthy perspective, and let me say something. By you coming to me, that lets me know you don't think this is a helpless situation and you want to get help. That is half the battle."

Something inside me withered away like a flower that knew its season has come and gone. I felt vulnerable. "It all comes from a place of wanting to do the right thing for my child."

"I understand. You are dealing with a lot and I know sometimes it can get hard to cope and the lines can get blurred How old is your baby?"

"He's eight months old." I smiled, pulling up his picture on my phone, as I thought about his laugh. His smile comforted me.

"He's beautiful! I have thirteen-month-old twins myself." She pointed to a picture on her credenza. "I understand that you feel your child is helpless and you want to do everything to protect him because I would do the same thing. I don't think that will ever stop, even when they are adults." She released a comforting laugh. "But your child is not helpless because you are his mother and you are here! Know that!"

Her comment strengthened me. "I know. Sometimes it's hard to take the high road when I'd rather scratch his father's eyeballs out when my child is returned in the way he is."

"What do you mean by 'the way he is'?" Ms. Clara looked at me more deliberate. I felt her instinct as a mother.

"Maybe I can best describe by example." I sat up as I spoke. "Jordan's on a feeding schedule and I provide the bottle because his father refuses to bother, but without fail, most if not all the bottles are returned and of course, without wonder the diapers are untouched since he's probably dehydrated and if he's wet, he's soaked with a rash in the original diaper he was in. So, needless to say, my child isn't his happy self, he's tired, uncomfortable and ravenous!" My eyes began to tear.

"Oh, dear! What does he say when you ask him why the baby wasn't fed?"

"He says he didn't cry, even though I've told him Jordan rarely does and doesn't fuss much as it is, especially if he is not comfortable. It took him almost three weeks to fuss at the daycare because he wasn't comfortable and he hardly sees his dad, so he's probably not comfortable with him. Thus the part about wanting to scratch his eyeballs out because he says it with a straight face, as though it's not a big deal."

"Poor baby! The baby's probably wondering why he hasn't been fed and he's confused where you are, but he probably also feels the difference between you and this man. Babies get it! Children get it! His dad will hurt himself in the long run because children don't forget when a negative association is formed or when there is no bond." Ms. Clara wanted to find consolation. "That would upset me to see my babies that way."

"I know! I can't stand it!" I balled up my fist. "Every time he's with him, I feel terrible, wondering if Jordan is going to sleep hungry and if he's okay. Next time, my attorney advised that I pick Jordan up with a friend to have a witness and to refrain from doing or saying anything other than the usual pleasantries. I find myself just needing the support and I don't want to break down!" I began to cry. "And I always bring at least three bottles when I pick him up, which he finishes before we can even get on the freeway in ten minutes." Ms. Clara stood up and walked to her desk to grab the Kleenex box. She held it out to me before setting it down on the end table to the side of my chair.

"I can understand how you feel and I think I would feel the same if I had to witness my children in that condition; or any child for that matter. When is the next visit?"

"I'm not sure, but I've refused visitation since I found out he forged my signature and took a million-dollar life insurance policy on my life," I said abruptly.

"Oh my gosh!" Ms. Clara said, with her hand to her mouth. "You said your attorney referred you. Are you in court yet?"

"Yes and visitation hasn't been established, but he still refuses to cancel the policy. I don't have to allow the visits until we go to court for our first hearing."

"How many visits had there been before you stopped visitation?"

"Only a few because I was trying to let him see his child, but I had no idea he did this."

"At least you don't have to allow visitation until you are in court. When is your hearing?"

"Our first hearing is in a few weeks, but the court requires you to go through three before you are granted a trial and they don't believe this is cause for an emergency hearing. That's where the insanity begins. I'm not sure if it's Clyde or the long court process that will drive me crazy first?" I felt helpless and suddenly became warm. My heart was racing.

"Have you missed a lot of time from work?"

"Yes and no. There have only been two visits, but both times when he returned from a visit he was upside down on his schedule. He was super clingy and restless for almost two weeks and at times screamed out at night." I paused. "He does get sick more that he's started daycare now, but I can manage that and get him on his feet in a day or two, but this knocks us both out for a few weeks."

"I understand how you feel and I know there is a light at the end of the tunnel for you by just your being here. I can tell you are a great mom. You are very intelligent and beautiful and you have a lovely child, which I know makes it all worth it." She was encouraging. "The external of a person is a reflection of their internal state of mind and their life is an outward picture of an inside condition. From what you are telling me, he may very well have some personal issues and I know you get mad, but don't give him the power to control you. Where does he stay when he is here?"

"I have no idea because he never tells me. He says it's none of my business!"

"The court should have an issue with that. I wouldn't allow visitation if I didn't know where my children would be. There is just no way!" She spoke, determined. She meant it.

I feel very blessed to have my baby, but some days it gets hard having to deal with this which is why I am here."

"I understand, and I know if you don't share someone's reality or perspective, it becomes increasingly difficult to relate to them, but you have to forgive him and forgive you and move forward because there are so many blessings coming. I just know it! What is his relationship like with his dad?" Ms. Clara changed the subject.

"I don't believe he had much memory because he told me he died when he was an infant."

"What about his relationship with his mom?"

"He didn't talk about her much and when I met her, their interactions were awkward. I know he calls her by her first name."

Ms. Clara sat listening intently. "Really? Is that his mother by birth?"

"As far as I know." I shrugged my shoulders.

Ms. Clara sat listening intently. "That's the first level of disrespect for sure, when a child calls his mother by her first name. Her allowing it also says a lot, but that's another story. What do you mean by 'their interactions were awkward'?" Ms. Clara tilted her head.

"He waited on her and she always carried on about him as if he could never do anything wrong and they always seemed to be inside each others' personal space when they talked."

"Interesting. Sounds endearing of sorts. They seem to behave from a place of guilt and possibly fear, which can be interesting dynamic between parent and adult child. I'm not sure who has either, if they do, but some entitlement or narcissism could form from there. A lot of parents believe their children can do no wrong, but it can be unhealthy for the children growing up without consequences or boundaries. I'd like to think he's being a gentleman, but that seems contradictory if he also refers to her by her first name and how he behaves with you. His mother may have some guilt since she was a single mom and he didn't grow up with a father. Did his mom remarry and have any more children?"

"If she did, he never talked about a step dad. I'm not sure how many siblings he has." I presumed dismissively.

Ms. Clara nodded contemplative. "So what are you trying to accomplish in court?"

"Besides sanity, I want to establish visitation and child support." I exhaled, as I thought of the exhausting process. Though hearing those words, I didn't understand why it had to be such a process and be so complicated. My thoughts went to Candace and Abigail and lemonade.

"Hopefully court can help bring some closure to this for you and at least put some parameters on the visitations with respect to times and maybe even supervision for now as it doesn't sound like he's interested in the child's routine and needs." Ms. Clara offered. "How long does your attorney think the process will take?"

"She said it could be up to a year. The court moves at a snail's pace because everyone is on the same calendar and the system is just more and more delayed. You'd think with the divorce rate as high as it is now they would attempt to change the laws and rules that were implemented centuries ago to accommodate the changing times."

"Bless your heart! That sounds agonizing when a little one is involved," Ms. Clara said sympathetically. "We need to focus on getting closure for you. How do you think we can achieve that?"

"Unfortunately, I don't think there is any closure with this guy. I think it is more a matter of how I deal with it and I have reconciled that I have to believe the court will do what it is supposed to do to protect my child."

"That's probably a true statement if what you are telling me about him is true, but we're going to also focus on closure for you and that will help you to navigate through this without the volatile emotions. You can't give him the power in your life," she professed. "Were you guys married?"

"Heck no! I had some sense! Which is why this system is even more preposterous because I am going through the same length of process as if we were and no one is debating paternity!"

"That's disappointing and concerning because a child is caught up in it. You're doing what every mother should do and you need to focus on that beautiful baby." She paused, composing her thoughts. "If we change the way we look at things, the things we look at begin to change. And, I will tell you, the first step in wanting to change is seeking help and knowing when you need it and the second step is faith with work."

"I am trying and that's why I am here."

"I think the best thing for us is to explore some of the decisions you made to get you where you were and where you are now, and then we'll discuss how to move forward. This was a great first session. We covered a lot of background and it's a good place to stop to be able to process and think about what we talked about and questions you may come up with now and along the way that you may want to confront." She paused, clasping her hands together. "We can meet every few weeks or every week or just leave it open. Whatever works for you?"

"I just want to do what is right for my child and learn the best way to cope in the process." I smiled. "I think I'd like to start weekly and adjust as I think I need, if that's okay? I just really need to talk and get this out because it's getting overwhelming with the court process also."

"That works for me." Ms. Clara smiled, nodding with confirmation. "Does same time next week work then?" I nodded.

We both stood and bid our good-byes until next week. I felt relief meeting Ms. Clara like there was a light at the end of this tunnel, as she suggested.

"I'm going to be okay," I whispered under my breath, as I squinted stepping outside into the bright sunshine. I rummaged in my purse for my sunglasses.

I heard the faint idling of a car in the parking lot, as I got in my car and started it up. It was a loud, heavy engine. I looked forward to picking Jordan up.

Our first hearing was not for a few weeks. My attorney and I didn't know if or who Clyde's representation was, as we didn't get any response to our original process of service. This from the same guy who lived his life from not one, but five post office boxes. Clyde liked to work himself up into his own secrecy and give himself alias persona names. He called it being private. I had no idea what that was about.

I recalled one of Clyde's college friends that I had met that warned me to steer clear of Clyde advising that his world could implode at any given instant. I didn't ask details. He didn't tell. I listened.

⟨⟩

"Just think, Olivia, you could still be in Chicago and you could still be with him. You didn't waste time. You suspected he had some serious issues and you high-tailed it out," Madison offered. "Do you know how many women would have stayed because they felt like they had to and turned a blind eye or because they, in some deranged way, thought they could change him of his ways?"

Madison and I had met the first day starting undergrad, while we waited in line to register. Walking straight up to me, she asked my name and told me she had a crush on my boyfriend and, although I wasn't sure how to take her statement, I knew we would always be in one another's lives in some way or form. I have to admit, I liked her directness. Our friendship grew comfortable over the years. We could talk every day or every six months, picking up where we left off the last time, never missing a thing. A few years older than me, she was soft spoken and timid. I admired the gentle spirit she carried and her sense of tolerance because I didn't possess those qualities; knowing often we are attracted to that which we lack. She was attractive, with her petite stature and mocha brown skin; she always wore her hair in the latest fashionable style off her shoulders and kept up with the latest trends. I admired her determination to follow her dream to become an established surgeon and she admired mine for finding myself in life other than school, at least not what I went to school for.

She was in Charlotte for a conference and we met for some lunch in between her sessions. I decided to take the day off for a much needed 'me' day. We sat at a table next to the window. The lunch crowd was thinning.

"You know me. I know better than to think I can change a man, and I definitely won't compete with other women!" I spoke with a reflective tone.

"I still can't believe it. I just can't believe it. I mean you moved while you were pregnant?" I wasn't sure if she was being cynical or sympathizing because her tone was unattached and unemotional. She was delicate with her mannerisms and every word she spoke.

We were both hungry and ready to order. I, the meatloaf with fries and a sweet tea, and Madison, a burger with fries and a Mountain Dew. Not much had changed since college when she'd drink Mountain Dews to stay up to study, while I napped with the textbook under my pillow after staring at the pages long enough, honing my photographic memory and growing cross-eyed.

"You know I never speak in regret, so I'm definitely not going to start now with the most amazing blessing of a child, but I still can't help but feel embarrassed and ashamed for even associating with this guy. I had a child for heaven's sake. It's not like I took his life," I said with exasperation, throwing up my hands.

"He probably looks at it like you did! You broke it off with him and now he's in court. He probably thought he got away with everything he did and he might even be afraid some things will be exposed. Sadly, I think it's just begun for you." Madison had a sad look. It seemed like something was on her mind, but Madison was never comfortable if you asked questions. She would talk to me when she was ready. If she ever was. "I remember when he told you he wanted no part of you or the baby when you found out you were pregnant, but you never wavered in your decision."

"It was never about him." I didn't want to cry again. *I am strong,* I told myself.

"True! I get that now being in my own situation with Howard. I'm learning what doesn't break you makes you stronger. We're still here and we're doing quite nicely, Olivia. You inspire me! Jordan is an incredible child and you only have yourself to be proud of for that. His dad, on the other hand, just wants to make you miserable. Don't let him!" she exclaimed.

"Oh you need not worry about that." I smiled.

"God allowed this to happen because He knew we could handle it. This didn't happen *to* us, Olivia, it happened *for* us and He doesn't put more on you than you can handle. I know what you've been through before and that was just a preparation for this. I know you are going to be fine through this. You can do this. Jordan will get that, too, if he doesn't already with a mom like you. I hope Rachel will too. Speaking of Jordan, how is he doing?"

"He was such a good baby and now, he's an easy toddler. I am so blessed! I keep waiting for the nightmare stories people talk about, but like I said to my mom, 'God takes care of babies and fools' so, we're covered!" I chuckled. The waiter brought our food.

"You're one of the strongest women I know and I am not saying that to make you feel better. I mean it! I don't know what I would have done if I were in your shoes with all the added stuff like the life insurance policy and the lies and not having my family close. Howard just walked away from day one. I'm proud of you."

Madison and I maintained our friendship through all the changes, including with each other, that both our lives had taken in good balance; Madison's gentler manner always softening whatever situation, and myself being more rough around the edges, abrasive and tell it like it is. We had been there for each other when we needed to talk during challenging times in our lives; times that bonded our journeys with understanding, patience and forgiveness, while gently allowing each of us to grow.

"Thanks, girl, but it's funny to hear you say that only because I think the same of you! You're right on this happening *for us* and I feel so honored that it did!" I stopped myself and looked away, holding back the tears, as I often had these days. "We've gotta get the kids together and we have to stop talking about it. I'm so glad we could get out and catch up. I need more adult conversation and less lullabies some days." I chuckled. "I'm so jealous. You've got the perfect setup with your family close to help you. I don't trust anyone to babysit, not yet, even for a few hours."

"I am lucky and they are so helpful. We really should get the kids together." She paused, pointing to our plates. "I must say, you must be hungry because you are eating more than I think I've ever seen you eat."

"I guess I'm making up for when I'm either running after Jordan or too tired to eat." I shrugged my shoulders. The waiter sensed the energy of our conversation, not wanting to cause any interruption with his hand and head gestures.

"You look smaller than before your pregnancy."

"It's probably the stress of this legal battle. It's the newest weight loss program going and I *don't* recommend it!"

"No kidding!" We both laughed. "Maybe all that working out we did in college served us well. What are you doing the rest of the day?"

"My days are like a well-oiled machine between being a single mom, working, cleaning and cooking. In that order, but today I am going to the spa for a massage and then going home to cook dinner before I need to pick up little man. Okay, so not totally a me day then." I smiled.

"You have to take care of you or else we are no good to our kids."

"Amen! I'm learning." I raised my glass for a toast. We settled the bill, as we continued to chat.

We bid our good-byes until the next time.

As I sat in my car reflecting on the past year, trying to make sense of it all, remembering Madison's reminder that what doesn't break you makes your stronger. I wondered if the intended purpose of my current situation was for me to train for the Ironman or if God just has a great sense of humor. I decided wallowing in the whys would be futile and exhausting, and concluded that sometimes there's just no making sense of the senseless. For the record, I had no interest in training for the Ironman.

Nine
BEST INTERESTS

ANOTHER WEEK PASSED BEFORE OUR FIRST hearing, and I grew more anxious to get the responses to our Interrogatories before our court date. We condensed our questions to those relevant to anything that could be unsafe, confusing, and emotionally unhealthy to a child.

I couldn't help but question Clyde's character based on the lies he had told and some of which he didn't tell, but were revealed and discovered along the way and most certainly the forgery of the life insurance policy.

My mind raced as I did more research about different mental illnesses and my thoughts switched from sympathy to concern for many reasons. At minimal, I wished I had done it sooner to understand the chances of passing it to my child, as well as learning how to live with it. Clyde's temper could be set off in a moment's notice and for no reason at all; both of which added to the frustration when trying to communicate with him. A key behavioral trait in many conditions, I learned in my research, is not being able to be considerate of others or see reality the way the rest of the world sees it, which lends to more frustration and communication spirals out of control from there. With this background, it came as no surprise that Clyde had rarely been in a long-term, serious relationship from what he told me, if ever. Add an analogous personality of a narcissist to the equation, which can be very common for several conditions as well, and the chaos and madness heightens. I just didn't have much to go on from Clyde's description and, given the sensitivity of the issue, never asked any questions. I was simply going with a broad-brush stroke, trying to diagnose what possible conditions it could be based on his behavior. I became highly paranoid where my child's health was concerned.

I only saw a piece of Clyde's character and, from what I did see, I concluded I didn't need to know any more when I made the decision to exit. He was an incredible actor and had a great ability of masking or manufacturing emotions at a moment's notice, as I had witnessed so often to the point that I couldn't tell what was genuine and what was not like some sort of an addiction to manipulate and fool people for the sheer pleasure and control of it.

The day had finally come for our first hearing and I hadn't slept a wink the night before, which was becoming usual for me since learning of the life insurance policy and having to fight for my child's safety. It seemed criminal to have to fight for our safety, which should have already been within our rights.

I was anxious passing through the x-ray machines at the courthouse, as I fidgeted through my briefcase for my court notice to find the courtroom number.

Friends familiar with the legal process, for one reason or another, warned me that the system for civil matters is grey and, sadly, most visitation parenting plans orders are canned language that doesn't necessarily consider each situation individually and many parents are given visitation regardless of anything other than being parents.

I noticed my attorney waiting outside the courtroom looking up from her stack of papers, waving to me. She wore a navy suit and looked especially calm and rested.

As expected, Clyde and his attorney stonewalled and didn't produce the answers to Interrogatories and documents to be produced purposefully until thirty minutes prior to our hearing; still with extensive information missing; still non-compliant.

My attorney assessed which documents remained outstanding while I scanned over the Interrogatory responses, focusing on the questions that were of concern to me regarding my son's health and his father's history. In particular, I read and re-read the questions and answers to four particular questions having to do with Clyde's health, as I hoped to make sure I wasn't misunderstanding what I was reading.

Dropping the papers on the floor, I suddenly felt sick to my stomach clasping my hands over my mouth. My attorney motioned to me in the direction of the ladies restroom. After a few heaves, I slowly regained my strength and composure, not wanting to touch anything in the dinged stall. I stared in the mirror, blotting my mouth with a moistened paper towel. I pulled my suit jacket down, stood up straight affirming my calmness, and walked out. My attorney's eyes met with mine, as I walked toward her and resumed my seat.

"Are you okay? I should have read them first, but I just got them and didn't have a chance. You know I've always tried to protect you and I've even advised you to grow some thick skin in the process," Debra affirmed, nodding her head. "Now would be a good time to start." I glanced down. My body felt weak.

"Did I read them correct?" I asked quietly. I was confused and lost.

"You did." She appeared perplexed. As I gazed around, there were a few other clients huddled with their attorneys. The attorneys seemed composed and poised, while their clients seemed bewildered and exhausted. I was both the latter. My attorney the former.

"I don't know what to believe now. I want to shout, but I can't and I want to cry, but my eyes sting because they are dried out and there are no tears left," I said helplessly.

"We just have to find the truth and I'm going to help you do that. There is something wrong with him!" I could see it in her face that she was disturbed and she was strategizing in her head.

I had nothing left inside me. I was numb. "It's as if he's playing a game just to mess with you."

The bailiff called our case. We gathered our things and entered the room on the side of the courtroom. He was a tall average-sized man, as I considered the likelihood of his ability to take Clyde had he gotten out of control, not to mention the weapon tucked neatly in his holster. I collected myself, whispering the words under my breath, "I can do all things through Christ who strengthens me." The judicial officer was seated, sorting through some papers. She paused to say hello, exchanging idle conversation with my attorney. She was a middle-aged woman with short hair that was completely grey and facial lines that gave her an exhausted, but distinguished appearance.

"I can feel your distress." Debra put her hand on my forearm, as she bent closer to me to speak quietly. "Not that it lessens it in any way, but this is why we are here and I promise I will do everything I can to get to the bottom of this for you and Jordan. I don't know what kind of a person does these things?"

"I'll be okay." I felt a chill come over me, as my body shuddered, remembering the past year of my life. *I am strong.*

"He also still hasn't produced the requested documents and definitely not the ones that could incriminate him further, which tells me he has a lot to hide." Debra paused, looking up from the stacks of papers she had sorted through. "He's playing games and wants to run up your bill and that's fine because he'll end up paying them, too. The judge doesn't take kindly to this type of stonewalling," Debra said confidently, as she sat up straight and wrote a few notes.

"It scares me to think what else he is hiding and I don't know if we've even touched the surface."

"I don't know if you ever will really know someone like him. You just keep Jordan the focus and let God do the rest."

"I'm just here to protect my child! Nothing more, nothing less!"

"Trust me on this one!" Debra grabbed my hand, giving it a gentle squeeze. I felt encouraged, although my body felt as though it would collapse if the back of the chair weren't holding me upright.

The bailiff reappeared, interrupting to tell us that opposing counsel was back and meeting with her client in the hallway.

"Jordan will get it as children always do. I do understand. Hang in there. One's ship comes in on a calm sea." I thought of Trevor.

I heard Clyde's voice in the hallway, as he and his attorney walked around the corner. He wore a smug face.

Debra exchanged the cordial small talk pleasantries with opposing counsel, as she sat down. My stomach was in knots. I gave the obligatory smile and looked away. *I was glad I had not eaten a heavy breakfast earlier.*

We stated the issues to the judicial clerk. She listened to both sides, asked a few questions and made a few facial expressions of unbelief with raised eyebrows, shaking her head periodically. She spoke unemotionally with an almost dismissive regard. Perhaps her years of hearing cases made her appear as such. Clyde managed to squeeze out a few tears for good measure, though I wasn't affected since I'd witnessed them before, as he told lies of his health history a year prior, learning just minutes prior it had all been a sham. At his urging, and more tears, Clyde pleaded that the judge assign a Guardian Ad Litem, as he played his classic victim role, although he couldn't substantiate any basis for his claims. I was sickened to hear the judicial advocate not only grant his request, but she also allowed a supervised visit with Jordan in a few weeks, citing that it had been two months since his last visit since I had canceled visitation after learning of the insurance policy, as if it were my fault. What was more disturbing was the proposed supervision was to be with Clyde's elderly aunt, and that it would only be for the first visitation, although there would be several visits between now and possibly up to a year until we were put on the trial calendar. The thought alone made me cringe, as I wondered how a court felt a family member could remain objective, let alone an elderly family member. Short of appearing unreasonable or overly protective and at my attorney's advice, I had no choice, but to reluctantly defer to the court in this matter. A court that seemed to clearly show bias and poor judgment. The judicial advocate also granted child support and offered two free opportunities to mediate in an attempt to resolve our issues. The satire to that was I would have attempted to reason with Clyde. In fact, I would have preferred it and saved myself the preposterous amounts of money the legal fees were costing me, had there been some opportunity outside of forgeries for a life insurance policy or falsifications of a death certificate and health condition or even the opportunity for a conversation devoid of insults.

I had come to the court looking for some truth since I couldn't make sense of it and, in the least, to find some reasoning, although none was found at this early stage, but in the meantime, temporary visitation was granted with no questions asked or caution taken.

I was outraged at the court and the judicial officer's position for not erring on the side of caution and pushing us along the court process, while an innocent infant was subject to a father's questionable interest, at best, given what had occurred. At the court's minimal discretion, it failed to recognize Clyde's contemptuous and fraudulent behavior, discretion that should be required of the court to protect a child's best interest.

It was my opinion that both parents, even devoid of any questionable or illegal behavior in their past or present, but especially with documented questionable behavior, should have to submit to a psychological evaluation, an alcohol and drug screening and a full blown background check for the courts to assess before anything less than supervised or only day visits are granted in a registered neutral facility with the transgressing parent. After all, you do these screenings to secure many jobs, minus the psych evaluation. But, wasn't caring for a child given any special consideration compared to employment? Unfortunately, for me, I was learning the court's opinion was different and a parent is considered innocent until proven guilty where children are concerned. Judicial officers only involve themselves to the extent they want to get involved, in the name of preserving the best interest of the child. That same child that otherwise doesn't have a voice, especially in the meantime when and until the lengthy court process presents the time to be heard by the judge. That is what the courts claim to do, but then again, that's the satire of the process.

More troubling to me is that some states have very different guidelines; many stricter, some more moderate, but I wondered why the geographic location of a child mattered since their well being should be the same in North Carolina or California and everywhere in between. I thought the state laws should be more uniform in an effort to weed out the variation and the possibility to manipulate the system that is already vulnerable to legal loopholes and lobbyists; a system, ironically, that was founded in the name of justice and a system that is supposed to protect children equally everywhere. Those same children that cross state lines many times before they are adults.

I believe courts shouldn't remain impartial where children are involved and especially when there is question. I do think the court needs to act from a place of bias in favor of protecting innocent children endowed with a future, especially when one or both of the parents do not and especially when anything can be proven, but that is also just my opinion. To that same opinion, the future of our children is far too precious to be thrown in the middle of the court battle where common sense and sound reasoning has been misappropriated and abandoned.

Needless to say, there was nothing accomplished in the hearing more than what we came to court knowing were the issues and as part of the process, the county I resided in required two more hearings at least thirty days apart before a trial date would be granted in front of the judge, though visitation was granted in the meantime.

I recognized it was a big money making process for the court system that proceeded at a snail's pace and in grave need of resources while innocent children were subjected to standard and customary visitation in almost every circumstance short of proving sexual or physical abuse, which also has its own challenges to prove in court. The delay itself was in direct contradiction to the best interest of the child, when temporary injunctions or rulings are not made. Rulings that can be and should be made by judicial officers, but choose to appear impartial. I realized my opinions meant nothing and I felt helpless.

It should have been my first indication that the court would act with a blatant misdirection of everyone's resources and prolonged proceedings since Clyde and I were subject to the same lengthy process of law for having dated only three months, as someone who had been married for forty years. And, although 40.8 percent of babies born in the United States in 2010 were delivered by unwed mothers, compared to 5.3 percent in 1960, the antiquated laws were still written from the past and in desperate need of changing to uniformly protect children and single parents to shorten that process, leaving time for when essential and extended proceedings are necessary in more contentious cases to focus on the children that need the legal system most.

I'm not sure if Clyde's stonewalling in these legal proceedings, his litigious delays or his inconsistent visits were his attempts to inconvenience me, as he probably hoped, or it was a lack of interest, finances or time. But, I was determined to fight and show the court that Clyde's selfishness and lack of sincerity should be considered where a child's best interest is concerned, and that parenting is not designed by convenience and nor should visitation be granted by paternity. It seemed that I couldn't, in any way, convince the court that if a person went to such great lengths that Clyde did to attempt to dissuade me from having a child with attempted forgery, misrepresentation and fraud, we could in no way know he was sincere and if he would protect the child's well being, at least not without more information. Sad and disturbing as Clyde's behavior was, I couldn't comprehend or excuse it under any circumstances, even under the pressure he may have felt as he presented, but I had to live with it and took solace in knowing it would all work out because of my faith.

Clyde and my communication regarding Jordan and his wellness, routine or visitation concerns had been minimized to Clyde's continual onslaught of insults with a determination to do anything and everything I had suggested in an opposite manner, always being met with resistance and contention. I wasn't sure whether to feel compassion for him because he really had no clue or to be angry for his clear neglect and selfishness regarding caring for my child. Again, I opted to defer to the process of the court system to bring some clarity to an otherwise troubling situation. Clyde's attacks were of a deliberate, venomous and retaliatory kind, which made me believe that everything he did was premeditated and predictable and even in the midst of deflecting the pain that Clyde so vehemently inflicted, directly and indirectly, I was overwhelmed with peace; peace that was borne from my pain. My peace gave me the strength and the focus I needed to fight the fight worth fighting with a peace to persevere and to stay the course.

In some way, I wished I could protect Jordan and shelter him at such a young, tender age, but I found solace knowing children always do figure it out as I'd been told countless times when parents only sting themselves when they have ill intention and spew negativity rather than love. I trusted Jordan would be stronger and wiser for all that was happening.

I was determined to give Jordan full access to whatever he was interested in and that he would feel no different than his childhood friends raised in a home, with a mother and a father, under one roof, in the same way so many men had been raised by single mothers, living life being good men and achieving great happiness and success.

My faith was securely grounded. Even though Clyde tried to project misery into my life, I would not allow him to interfere with God's will on my life. My prayers strengthened my faith, bonded my trust and sustained my belief in myself to rise above it all; all of which gave me delight and pleasure with Jordan to enjoy our life.

"Can you believe that? He lied about his supposed child dying and he was still given visitation with his aunt?" I was settling in for the evening after putting Jordan to sleep though I was still very restless. "Where are you?"

"I'm out." Walter sounded vague. "Are you in for the night?" *It isn't like him to be vague,* I thought. *Maybe paranoia is setting in for me.*

"Sounds windy wherever you are. Yep, we're in." I heard Walter's car start up over the receiver. It sounded as though it were in stereo as I heard a car start up outside, too.

"Be sure and lock up. Damn! Wait, so he lied about the child dying or that he had a child?" Walter sounded angry, changing the subject.

"Both. There was no child and no one died. This court is making me crazy and I know I have to keep it all together, but this is my child." I didn't realize I was pacing until I turned and stepped on one of Jordan's toys.

"Damn! You're doing a great job and whenever you want to lose it, just look at that great little guy of yours and know it will all work out for good. It may not make sense at all right now, but it will and you've got to keep yourself healthy to enjoy all that is to come. I can't imagine how you feel, but know any compliments that come to your child, and they will, will all be because you loved him," Walter offered. "I'm so sorry. You don't deserve this."

"Thanks. I can hear my attorney in my mind telling me to take the high road and that it'll all work out, but sometimes it's hard to think that's possible where I am right now. And, I'm so tired from it all." I dropped myself down on the couch, reaching for the remote control. I contemplated having a glass of wine to unwind, but I desired sleep more than anything.

"Some people enjoy being miserable in their own misery and then when they get out of it, they create more. 'As a man thinketh, so does he perceive,' is his state of mind and his inward condition. I still can't believe the court granted supervision with his aunt though. Can you ask for another supervisor?" I was exhausted even considering the question. The television was watching me, as I sat motionless hearing most of what Walter was saying, but filling in a lot of blanks to catch up to the conversation.

"We have two more hearings before the trial in June and unless the court deems it an emergency or there is some material change, they won't grant another hearing or change what has been decided."

"Well, a family member is hardly unbiased and not much of a supervisor. How old is she? When is the next visit?"

"I'm not sure. That visit is next weekend and there's one more visit before our next hearing in a few months, but this is the only one supervised, if you can call it that. He fought so obsessively in our hearing for visitation every few weeks, but he's already canceled in advance and pushed back the next hearing!"

"Well damn, what has to happen for them to consider it an emergency and isn't the purpose of supervision to make sure the visits are without incident? How can the court only determine he only needs one visit supervised? I guess that's the system. Don't the courts realize you have nothing to gain by interfering with his visits, but that the child has everything to gain by being safe and cared for?" He sounded enraged. "That's the court's job at the least. All his cancels should at least speak to his intentions and he damn sure shouldn't be allowed to ask for extensions, especially this far in advance." He sighed.

"I don't know what the court is doing or this judicial officer. Unless I personally witness physical abuse, my attorney says they'll just continue the status quo like some math equation for all the cases that come to their court."

"That's probably why so many people falsely claim abuse because they probably know that's what it takes to get their attention. They should know neglect and alienation is abuse to a child's emotional and mental well being also! And how can the court consider a child safe if the visiting parent doesn't even tell you where your child stays and he won't even take your calls when he has the child? This sounds like they're looking for 'a reasonable doubt' in a criminal case. When it's a child, it's a reasonable doubt. No questions asked." I heard the quiet stillness of the night with the television muted. It was almost eerie.

"Well, I think we have 'reasonable doubt' several times over since he, himself, admitted to lying in his Interrogatories in our first hearing. I know they can't really believe this is in the best interest of the child since that is what they claim to protect. I worry every minute Jordan is with Clyde, yet I'm the one in court defending myself," I said, angrily walking back to check on Jordan sleeping peacefully in his crib. I was exhausted.

"There's enough to worry about just being in the least, a parent, trust me. A parent shouldn't ever have to wonder where their child is when they are with the other parent. I had to tell my parents where I was as long as I was still living under their roof and out late, and the way I see it, if one parent doesn't tell the other parent where their minor child is, he shouldn't be allowed visitation. Heck, maybe they should make the laws to protect the rights of the other parent from alienation?" he exclaimed.

"Definitely when a parent wants to spite the other parent." I felt myself growing frustrated.

"No kidding! I know from my costs and probably yours, too, we could have sent our kids and a few others to college with the thousands of dollars we spent on attorney's fees. That is crazy!"

"And I just dated him three months. At least you were married! It's like the court punishes you for coming to them!"

"There is probably some truth to that to make it worth their time for having to be involved, including the attorney's interest, but the facts are still the facts. You'd have to be blind and deaf to deny the facts of your case. Hopefully, he'll have to pay your attorney's fees, too."

"I just have to manage my reaction to things and make the most peaceful and happy life for Jordan and I. I sometimes still wish he'd follow up on the offer he made to me months ago and save us both the agony."

"Something tells me he won't because he sees so much in Jordan now and he'll want to take some of that credit. He enjoys making you miserable in the process, too, and this way he can still have you in his life, too. I think it's pathetic that he claims that you're the one not over him yet, he's the one that carries on like he's scorned. He's clearly not over you. Everyone can see that," Walter attested.

"Have him tell it, I'm the one that tried to trap him, but then he'll claim I'm the one that abandoned him. It all makes my head spin, really."

"That's why everyone gets it; everyone, but him, that is. Hey, I was thinking that I have to be on that side of town tomorrow, so I could bring you and the little guy something to eat. I know you're probably exhausted working double time since getting back to work and you could catch a break from cooking dinner. Just an idea." I immediately felt Walter's comfort and was feeling more sleepy now.

"You are so considerate to do that. I will take you up on that. Tomorrow works fine. I have an appointment with my therapist, but we should be home after five."

"Now that you are locked up. Get some sleep."

"Sleep?" I chuckled. "I think until trial that is a thing of the past." I sighed.

Ten
WISDOM

MS. CLARA ANNOUNCED SHE WAS READY for me, as she motioned for me from down the hall to come on back. She resumed her seat, as we entered her office. I smelled the subtle scent of jasmine in the air.

"Anything new with the court?" She hesitated, as if she forgot something. That's how I felt most days.

"No!" I sat down on the couch. "We had our first hearing and there's a visit coming up next week."

"How are you doing?"

"Each day is stressful just communicating with Clyde, but I'm doing the best I can."

"You gave me some background on the last visit and I want to continue there and then you can catch me up to what happened in the hearing." She paused, taking a sip of her water. I reached for the bottle on the side table she always had waiting for me. "Let's go back to when you met your son's father and what you thought was unsettling about him that may have given insight to his character and where you were in body and mind during it all?"

I pondered her question as I swallowed. "I thought he was awkward and his conversation was superficial and I remember thinking he was very persistent and vain."

Ms. Clara was nodding. "Were you attracted to him?"

"Actually, no," I said matter of fact.

"Why and when did you start dating?"

"About a month later I accepted his repeated invitations. I think I was just bored and thought maybe a long distance relationship could be manageable since I could choose when I would see him. I realize that sounds bad, but it's where I was at the time and I didn't want to be in a relationship." I stopped. "I guess it was the kiss."

She looked surprised. "I've heard a lot of things before, but what was it about a kiss that would make you ignore all the things you weren't attracted to?" She paused. "I'm inquiring so you can articulate what it was, to understand how you got there. You've already said you were not interested and there was something awkward about him, but what made you turn left when all the signs at the fork in the road were pointing right?" She sounded stern now. I felt reprimanded, like from my mother. I stared out the window, looking for any pleasant distraction.

"Truthfully, I just hadn't been kissed that way and just didn't think about all the other stuff. I thought I was in control."

"That's when the universe will remind you who really is in control. And, when we don't confront our issues, our issues will follow us until we do. Do you think you had any expectations?"

"Beyond the expectations of a man being a man, no, but I was open to finding out more about him."

"And what did you find out about him?"

"He's a 'can't do' man."

"Okay. What's that?" She asked hesitantly.

"It's probably easier to explain a 'can do' man because I've had those boyfriends. Clyde is completely opposite, which is why it's hard to imagine this happened. A 'can do' man makes a woman feel special and most importantly, that woman doesn't have to ask. He protects her, inspires her to be more and he manages his own success. He shares your dreams and even helps around the house and with the kids and yes, there's chemistry and you are attracted to him, too. Clyde was just a can't-do-a-darn-thing man, sitting around talking about nothing, but himself, playing the victim and taking more than he ever gave."

"Never heard it put that way, but that's interesting," Ms. Clara admitted. "But, you do know, no one is perfect, right?" She glanced at the clock that sat over the door in direct view of her chair.

"I do. Heck, I'm not perfect, but I want something to work with," I reasoned, brushing my hair away from my face.

"I get it and I think those are good standards to have. If someone can't bring you more of anything where you are and love you, then you have a choice to manage on our own." Ms. Clara nodded approvingly. "Did you feel lonely or alone?"

"No, neither. Bored is the best way I can explain it," I said, reflectively looking out the window. The sky gave me clarity of thought.

"Okay, that's fair. When you began spending time with him, did your thoughts change?"

"No, it just confirmed it for me. I remember thinking that the relationship would play itself out being long distance. I actually felt guilty thinking I wanted to break it off with Clyde because he claimed he loved me." I rolled my eyes.

"And you didn't believe him?"

"It had only been a few months so, I was surprised for sure. Then I found out he cheated on me around the same time, so what's love got to do with it?" I faintly chuckled. I was sarcastic.

"How did you find that out?" She had a puzzled look on her face. I remember that was the way I felt when I found out.

"I was on a last minute business trip and ended up sitting beside a guy that did some business with Clyde. That is, until Clyde had an affair with his ex and she gave Clyde personal information. Sounded like a mess! I don't know much more than that."

"Really?" Silence hung in the air. "Well, everything happens for a reason and you clearly needed to take that last minute trip. How did that make you feel when you found out?"

"Honestly, I felt betrayed, but I was relieved to have a way out finally, but I still felt humiliated that another person, a stranger, had to tell me what I ignored since day one." I looked out the window and noticed the seasonal flowers outside that speckled the garden with random color. Seasons. Changes. Growth. I took a deep breath.

"That's how the universe works. Did you confront Clyde?"

"No, I knew he'd just try to deny it and I really was just relieved. I broke it off with him when I got home that evening. I just told him I'd been thinking."

"Do you think you loved him?"

"No. I know I didn't. I remember when he told me he loved me, I felt awkward and I couldn't think of anything else to say except, 'Thanks.'" I was animated. I felt relaxed.

Ms. Clara chuckled. "That must have been awkward. I get it! When did you find out you were pregnant?"

"About three weeks later."

"Wow, so one door was slammed shut and another was opened, literally! Do you remember how you felt when you found out you were pregnant?"

"That's exactly what I thought! I felt numb, initially, because I had the most beautiful creation growing inside of me by a man I didn't love."

Ms. Clara was nodding in affirmation. "That happens more than we care to admit or believe, but many people are so caught up in the emotions of being pregnant and having a child that they think a baby will make the problems disappear. Another reason why our divorce rate is what it is," she said candidly. "Did you want to be pregnant?" The question sounded odd to me. Questions of this sort always made me uncomfortable, as if there was a plan.

"Want was a relative term then because, even though it happened, I didn't plan it and I didn't want to be pregnant with a guy I just broke up with three weeks prior and had no interest in being in a relationship with. So, I can't say I wanted to be pregnant, but once I found out, I was happy. I didn't really believe I was for a long time."

"Really? How do you not believe you are pregnant?" She sat back in her chair, as if getting comfortable and expecting more to the story.

"I didn't know if one brand of pregnancy test was more accurate than another or if they had expiration dates, but I bought four different brands of pregnancy tests to make sure." I chuckled. "And even after all the plus signs showed up, like I hit the jackpot on the slot machine, I still wasn't convinced for a long time because I had no symptoms and I didn't gain weight for five months. I was very blessed to have a great pregnancy." My mind reminisced.

"Sounds like it! Consider yourself one of the lucky ones. Some of us are not that lucky," Ms. Clara claimed in her own recollection of what she had shared, a not so easy pregnancy with twins. "Did you think you were ready for a baby?"

"I was scared, but I read every book I could get my hands on about pregnancy and babies and I did everything I could to stay healthy. I worked out like crazy, though that was more to relieve stress. I slept a lot, too. I wanted to be a good mom."

Ms. Clara was smiling. "Take me through the feelings at that moment when the plus signs appeared."

"I was in shock, but I was at peace, too. That moment was a major game changer for me!" I paused. "I remember sitting frozen on the cold bathroom floor, hugging my knees tightly to my chest, whispering what seemed like a million verses from scripture and crying quietly. I was confused. I stayed there awhile just praying and being still, listening to my spirit and being remorseful that it took getting to that point to cry out to God for His unselfish love and guidance more than ever because I was lost." My eyes welled with tears, as I looked out the window at the courtyard. I remembered that time very clearly.

"Did you know what you were going to do?"

"I remember it was a cold morning, but I felt warm when I was crying, as though someone was hugging me and I felt comforted. I knew it was God and I knew it was His intended purpose fulfilled. I did know at that moment, without a doubt, I was going to have a baby. I was happy and I did feel like I hit the jackpot of sorts to be blessed to give life!" I smiled, brushing the tears away with my fingers that were now streaming down my cheeks.

"Can you describe your tears back then?" Ms. Clara passed me the Kleenex box from the end table beside her.

"They were tears of joy and pain because I didn't think it would happen this way with a man I had no feelings for and for the first time I also felt scared. I have never been scared like this in my life." I paused, as I choked up and began to sob. "I knew I would love my baby into this world and I wanted my child to be happy and proud for the reason they were brought into this world; to know undeniably that I was thankful and honored that God found favor with me to bless me with a child."

"Your child will know that, even if he doesn't now because he's young, but he will because you thought that much about him before he even got here. And, when he forgets, and he will, he will have no choice but to know because that's who you are." Ms. Clara nodded her head, her eyes looking inside mine.

"I just want him to know God gave him to me to care for and love him and that's what's most important to me." I wiped my tears.

"You mentioned it was a game changer for you. What do you mean by that?"

"Just that my life would change and I had to live differently. Nothing specific, but now there would be a baby, a child to care for."

"That's fair." She contemplated. "Kids change things. Did you feel like you were giving anything up?"

"No, just a game changer as far as my priorities were concerned."

"Who did you tell first?" Ms. Clara moved on. She had a way of doing that when she got the answers she wanted.

"I actually told my ex-boyfriend first," I admitted. "I wanted to tell my mom, but she wasn't home and I waited to tell my dad since I was going to visit him in the next few weeks and decided to tell him in person."

"Interesting." She paused. "I have two questions. One, why the ex-boyfriend and two, how did your dad take it?" Ms. Clara prodded deeper, as she propped her elbow on her knee, cradling her chin with her hand.

"I'll answer in reverse. I still felt a little ashamed to tell my dad at forty, but he embraced me with complete and unconditional love though I know he wanted different for me. He didn't sound surprised, maybe because he already had four out-of-wedlock grandchildren. He was supportive and let me know he was there if I needed anything." I recollected my thoughts. "And I told the ex-boyfriend because I never brought closure to the relationship when I broke things off and I guess I felt that I wasn't fair to him, but we're still very close friends today." I spoke very matter of fact.

"I get that. You really are a thinker. I hear the thought process you take yourself through and I usually don't hear so much deliberation from people. You live very consciously and rationally." She looked more intense. "I can see you getting frustrated because you probably want to come up with an answer or a reason for everything, but sometimes, Olivia, there just isn't one and you have to be still and let your intuition guide you," Ms. Clara said firmly. "You also have to leave room for error because you'll continually disappoint yourself."

"I know," I said with resignation, twisting the Kleenex in my hands. "I'm very black and white and I don't handle other people's drama or problems and make them mine. That's the gray part I don't do well."

"How does that work for you?"

"I run away," I said helplessly.

"Sometimes the very thing you run from will keep running after you if you don't confront it!"

"Yes, I'm learning that and I'm also learning what I can't change." I began to feel uneasy.

"Did you ever think that you wanted to be a single mom?"

"That's a good question, and I've asked myself that several times when this happened, as though I willed it happen in my subconscious. I didn't think about it either way, but I did think if and when I got pregnant, I would be with someone even if we weren't married and it would have been a choice we made together. I never did have the married and pregnant with the white picket fence fairy tale in my mind and I sure didn't hear any clocks ticking, so I just didn't think about it and decided quite early on that if and when it happened, it would be God's plan. Maybe I did will for it to happen like this?" I pondered.

"Or maybe, God has plans we don't know about!" she exclaimed. "So, you were ready to be pregnant and have a baby then?"

"I wouldn't say that either because it wasn't planned, but I did know I wanted to be the best mom I could be now that I was pregnant."

"You mentioned, when you found out you were pregnant that you were in shock and at peace. Can you describe the peace?" Ms. Clara glanced at her watch.

"I had known that peace from when I'd been lost in a valley experience in the past. Everything ultimately worked out and it was the best thing that could happen, in hindsight. I knew everything would be okay this time, as well."

"God also makes a way where there is no way. Did you have any resentment for Clyde?"

"In all honesty, no, I knew this wasn't about him. That would have meant there was some unfulfilled expectation, but I never had any with him. I really just didn't want to be with him and I couldn't blame him for that."

"Would you do anything different?" Ms. Clara held a contemplative look.

"Not a thing!" I shook my head, lost in thought. "Now that I am in this drawn out, brain exhausting court system, there are some days I wonder if I ever should have said anything and made it easier for myself."

"That doesn't sound like you because that sounds a little selfish, but I hear a very compassionate person when I talk with you."

"I know, but I'm being honest," I said dismissively.

"You always sound like you process through everything and you think about consequences and what something looks like in the future. So you met, got pregnant and you lived in different cities, but then you moved to Chicago. What made you decide to move to Chicago if you didn't love him?"

"Clyde said he wanted to try and wanted to be around for the pregnancy and witness his son's delivery," I said defensively.

"But he could have moved to Charlotte if he really wanted to be a part of it and it's certainly cheaper to live in Charlotte than Chicago for a single mom. Why did you make the move?" She sounded critical. "Did he make more money than you?"

"I have no idea how much Clyde makes." I paused, regaining my composure. "I assumed Clyde had a thriving practice in Chicago. My company had a location in the city and it was just easier for me to relocate." I felt my neck getting tight and stretched it for distraction. Ms. Clara sensed my uneasiness.

"Do you think he should have been the one to move, especially since you were the one who was pregnant?" she asked pointedly. I was silent.

"I never stopped to think about it. I just did it!" I exclaimed, throwing my hands in the air. I felt my heart begin to flutter, as I grew heated. "I didn't feel it was my right to take that away from him just because I didn't want to be with him, and at the time I didn't know what I know about him now."

"Did you have a conversation about who should move?"

"Of course we talked about it and he told me it would be harder for him to move because of his practice, but if I moved he could help me with the baby when I traveled," I said helplessly. "It just sounded like it would be better that way."

"But you said he cheated on you so what made you want to believe that it would be different and decide to move while you were pregnant? Did he help you with the move?"

"No, he didn't help me with the move and I didn't want to be with him!" I exhaled. "I gave him the benefit of the doubt, okay, and I thought maybe the baby changed him to want to do what was right. Why are you riding me, as if it's my fault for doing what I thought was right?" I hastily stood up and stormed toward the door. Ms. Clara rose from her chair.

"I'm not riding you, but part of getting help is exploring the reasons for why we do what we do and take responsibility for our actions, so we don't repeat them." Ms. Clara was calm. I stopped. "There is not a right or wrong thing that you did here, but we need to explore what you were thinking or thought you could change about him." I faced the door, as I took a deep breath.

"I didn't think I could change him. I just thought I was doing the right thing for my son to know his dad." I spoke defensively, as I turned around. "I didn't want him to move and then have to hear about it when I didn't want to be with him. It was just easier for me to move."

"I understand that, but why were you the one that moved?"

"I don't know." I shook my head, throwing my hands up. I felt confused when it all happened; then and now, and just couldn't explain it.

"Do you want to leave or do you want to continue and face your foe?" Ms. Clara sat down. She was her usual calmly poised self.

I slowly stepped towards the couch.

"Come sit." She gestured her hand for me to join her. She meant well and I knew my healing would dig deep in my sores. I tried to think of running to escape.

"I just didn't think I could face the day, if it ever came, and risk my son being mad at me if I didn't give his father that opportunity," I blurted out, sobbing. "He may have never forgiven me and I don't think I could live with myself if that happened."

"I understand that. Okay, so you felt guilty?" Ms. Clara softly concluded. "Sometimes, our actions are driven out of our emotions and if we can contain our emotions, then we can think clearer and make better decisions in the future."

"I just didn't want my child to think I was a monster for not letting his father be involved," I whispered, reaching for another Kleenex.

"There is nothing wrong with that. I like your thoughts and you are very compassionate," Ms. Clara said sympathetically. "Do you still think that way?"

"No. Jordan will know I did what I needed to do at the time and he will know his father for whoever he is." I spoke solemnly. "Maybe I shouldn't have moved to Chicago."

"Very good progress." She nodded. "Tell me about the hearing." She changed the subject. She had reached the answers she was after. The answers of mine to confront my foe.

"He was granted visitation, but only the first visit is supervised with his elderly aunt," I said frustrated, wiping my nose with the Kleenex.

"Having his aunt supervise seems biased and inappropriate. I would think since the facts are undetermined, a court would maintain the best interest of the child until the truth is established and steer more on the side of being careful rather than take any chances."

"I know. That is what everyone thinks, except the courts. It's completely outrageous to me that they even allowed any overnights with all the things he's done. The courts try to remain impartial, but with kids I think they need to exercise some partiality!" I exclaimed as I felt anger build up inside me though the sadness tempered me.

"Was anything else decided?"

"Child support," I said, disgusted.

"How often will the visits be?"

"He was given every few weeks, but he's already told me he'll probably only take visits once every few months. He just fought in the court for appearance sake."

"You would think that means something to the courts when a parent only sees such a young child every few months and that would be reason for no overnights."

"It doesn't. They don't get it."

"Less frequent visits could be more traumatic since Jordan is so young and doesn't have the memory capacity since the visits are far apart. His dad is like a stranger to him and he has to reacquaint himself each time." I sensed her mind racing with concern. She was a mom. "Maybe they should add a provision that if he cancels, he forfeits overnights?"

I sighed. "The court won't change any prior decisions without an emergency hearing, and unless I witness physical abuse, they won't grant one."

"That's preposterous." She spoke adamantly. She was clearly upset. I thought any parent would be, or at least they should be if they want to call themselves a parent.

"I know." I had heard this before. I was growing restless.

"This is good progress and our time is up." I sensed her frustration. "How are you doing?"

"I'm sorry for my outburst, but sometimes I get overwhelmed. I still can't believe this is happening to me."

"I know it's hard and I understand," she reaffirmed. "You are on the right path. You have to believe that nothing is ever lost and it will be returned back to you."

"It already has been returned to me with Jordan."

Ms. Clara smiled nodding her head in confirmation. "It has been!" She paused. "Same time next week work for you?" She stood up slowly.

"Yes."

"Keep reminding yourself of that power to stand." Ms. Clara pointed a finger to the air.

"Thanks." I walked out of her office. *Power with direction,* I thought.

I noticed a black Escalade in the parking lot with very dark tinted windows that I recalled seeing a few weeks ago at the daycare. I felt uneasy, as I was reminded of the life insurance policy that existed, wondering if Clyde was capable of such things.

My thoughts lingered to Jordan, dinner and bedtime. In that order. Exhaustion was setting in.

Eleven
BELIEVE

THE FRIDAY CAME FOR CLYDE TO pick up Jordan for one of his few and far between visits. I managed to remain calm most of my day, telling myself it was hurting me more than it was hurting Jordan since he'd hopefully sleep most of the time, and that Jordan would know his father for whom he was sooner or later. Today just happened to be the sooner. I pondered what life looked like in eight or ten years from now, when a child comes into their own and begins to have their own questions, ideas and opinions. Some questions they ask, some they don't, but in the end, as so many others have said and I agreed, they do get it. He'd do a great enough job of showing his neglect by his own doing and I wouldn't have to say a negative word about him. I prayed beyond Jordan knowing his dad, whatever relationship they would have, I would be strong enough for the two of us and make up where Jordan needed me. When Jordan needed me.

Trevor was also visiting this weekend for a weekend out to relax. I was excited to see him for some much-needed attention and distraction from worrying about Jordan every moment; although I wasn't sure how much relaxing I'd be able to do.

There was a small part of me that wanted to reconnect in the socialite network as I was before in Charlotte prior to moving, but I had grown weary of the exhausting scene. Now that my priorities in life had obviously changed, just the thought of getting myself together to go out was not in the least bit interesting to me. Besides that, I had lost some extra twenty pounds and in desperate need of some shopping for clothes that fit.

I dressed up my jeans paired with a fitted white t-shirt and a short black jacket. I wore classic silver jewelry and sling-back black heels. My hair was curly for a fun change and light make up with a brush of shiny gloss to finish the look.

Trevor took the lead, as I preferred, insisting we were going out for a night on the town—a little dinner, maybe some dancing—and anything else my heart desired. I was initially flattered when Trevor introduced himself to me while I was in Chicago, but seeing him again, I was speechless watching his stately masculine figure approach me after speaking with the host of the restaurant. His unpretentious spirit made him so attractive to me beyond his smooth complexion and and low-cut wavy hair that lined his perfectly symmetrical face. I loved the way he was a perfect gentleman and handled everything when we were out. I finally felt like I could exhale. He was as perfect as perfect could be. Although I never prayed for a man and didn't believe in dreaming about intangible things, I did trust God was watching after me and sent me an angel in Trevor.

The restaurant was enchanting and cozy and Trevor was everything I remembered. I felt like an excited schoolgirl all prettied up for the date I had longed for all year. If for no reason at all, Trevor renewed in me everything in life I had once believed in and wanted to believe in again even after life had tried to beat me down. I realized the purpose of my past and present was to make apparent and reassure me that I'd find love in every way it is intended; love of self, love of my child, love of my family and love of others. I didn't know when I'd find love again, but I did know in my heart the universe would present the right person to me at the right time, in the right way and I would know. I knew.

"You look absolutely stunning tonight. I don't think I've ever seen jeans look so good. And, I can't get that smile out of my head or maybe I just want to keep it on your face!" Trevor said, leaning in close to my face kissing my forehead. "Motherhood agrees with you! You know, I think your smile is the single first thing that attracted me to you. And, of course, that waddle of yours." Trevor chuckled.

"I didn't waddle!" I said in a whiny voice, sticking out pouty lips. I was blushing from the inside out, glad that the lounge was too dimly lit to notice.

"I confess. That was it!" Trevor stared in my eyes. "Did I tell you it is so great to see you again? My time was cut short with you while you were in Chicago and I want tonight to last."

"Trevor, honey, thank you for taking me out and making me feel like a princess. I haven't felt like this in a long, long time.

I will try not to worry every minute about Jordan while we're out." I sighed.

"You can talk about or worry about anything you want to, just as long as it's with me. This is your night! You do know I couldn't stop thinking about you since you left, and maybe I shouldn't even be here, but I just had to tell you how I felt and that you touched me with your soul in a way that no one ever has. Olivia, I don't mean to sound cliché, but you have awakened me and what is even crazier is you were pregnant with someone else's child when you did, but I couldn't let you get away. You are a special person to me, but you really are just a special person!" Trevor brushed my cheek with the back of his hand and then stroked my hair behind my ear. I felt his warmth. The restaurant was romantic and the corner table was private.

"I'm sure you just felt sorry for the pregnant woman and wanted to be a Good Samaritan, in case I fell over being a little heavy up in front." I chuckled, as I rounded my hands around my belly, remembering when there was a protrusion extending from my midsection. I was smiling ear to ear.

The waiter returned with a bottle of wine, as he gestured to Trevor. Trevor held his hand out to me to allow for my inspection. The waiter uncorked it, and poured a taste into my glass. I swirled my glass, allowing the wine some breathing room, and took a small sip. Signaling the waiter to proceed, he elegantly poured our glasses and disappeared.

"Now you know my angle because I was going up for an award for helping a pregnant woman. Nice try, but hardly woman!" Trevor nudged me. "That's not even the start of it and to see you months later, I am reminded in so many ways how I feel alive when I am with you, not to mention your infectious wit. After getting to know you, I've got to say your spirit is the second most thing that attracted me to you."

"Tell me, what was the first thing again? I forgot." I looked at Trevor shyly.

"That smile...the one I want to keep on your face, at least until the sun comes up tomorrow," Trevor said confidently, as he caressed my chin with his long fingers; winking as he noticed the waiter returning with our entrees. Entrees, of which I don't recall ordering—roasted lamb, braised duck, mashed potatoes, sautéed spinach and beet salad—all of which Trevor knew I loved.

"I don't know what to say." I looked around the table in awe, as my eyes began to tear.

"Don't say anything. Just enjoy. I got you!" He feather-stroked my lips with his finger. "Eat up. I was thinking after dinner we'd go somewhere dancing, lounging or whatever we want to do. How about Sunset Club or Zebra, and we can go from there?" Trevor humbly changed the subject, sensing my gratitude.

I shook my head. "Look at you? You're in my town. What do you know about Charlotte?"

"When are you going to realize that I listen to you and I hear what you enjoy and your interests?" Trevor exhaled. "And by the way, you're not the only person that does your research. You are always doing for Jordan. Please let me do for you. This night is yours!" I felt like a princess. Trevor was my prince.

"I'm up for anything!" We proceeded to savor our entrees as we sipped our wine, laughing and conversing about everything and anything.

"If there is one thing you would do differently, if there is something, what would it be?" Trevor inquired.

"Maybe not moving to Chicago, but I never would have met you. Can I ask you the same question?"

"I never would have let you leave Chicago or I would have moved here with you to Charlotte," Trevor said point blank, as he continued eating only stopping to look me in the eyes. "Of course, that can still happen," he said matter-of-factly, as he swallowed.

"Yes, it can. Charlotte has lots to offer." I smiled.

"Ah, baby girl. I did my research." Trevor smiled, returning his fork and knife to his plate. He leaned over and kissed me on the forehead. "I already know I like it. I just wonder if it would like me, or even love me back."

My cheeks felt as though I was blushing enough to light up the room. "You know my life is crazy upside down with my son's father and this court mess right now, but I'd love if you were here."

"Just be open." Trevor reached across the table, and placed his finger across my lips. "I came a long way to spend the night with you and I want to savor every minute you are willing to spend with me, if it just means I can hold you in my arms and lay on a hammock, watching the stars."

My eyes started tearing again for I couldn't believe what I was hearing from a man that had been so unselfishly generous and kind to me. "You mentioned Sunset Club…I think they're doing Paris in the fall and they have a few hammocks, but you have to get there early to get one!"

"You think we should try to call and reserve one?" Trevor asked in an exaggerated tone.

"You are unbelievable." I jabbed his chest. "You didn't miss a thing, did you?" I smiled.

"This girl I met taught me that if you are going to do something do it first class and, most importantly, have a plan. I know who you are and what you like. You didn't think I was coming to town to visit the most beautiful girl I know and wouldn't bring my best game, did you?"

"I love you. Let's do it!" I leaned over to kiss Trevor, looking at him sensuously. His lips were warm. "That girl that told you that is pretty smart." I nodded coyly.

"She's brilliant! She also said something about creating memories, and she's hot, too." Trevor shot me a racy look, as he ushered the waiter to finalize the tab, as we talked and teased enjoying tastes of all the delectable food from each other.

"A picture may be worth a thousand words, but memories are priceless," we said almost in unison.

"Let's go make some memories, lady!" Trevor stood up and held out his arm to escort me out.

"I'd like that, Mr. Johnson." I gave Trevor the once over look, smiled and reached up proudly. I wondered if he felt my hotness. Now, my jeans seemed like a bad idea.

Every inch of my body was smiling, as we got in the car waiting outside to take us wherever we wanted for the evening and return us to the valet lot for my car. Trevor didn't want to lose a moment of time in traffic or driving, while we could be conversing and relaxing. Trevor spoke discreetly to the driver. His phone rang.

"I gotta take this," he said, looking at me and holding up his finger to hang back. I shooed him away with my hands, and climbed in the car. I heard his voice outside the car. The moon glowed brightly in the dark sky.

"Yes, I'm in town. Good to know it's been quiet. You're back in town next week?" He paused. "I just have to be sure while this craziness is going on. Thanks, man. I owe you one. I appreciate your help. Hit me up next week when you're back in Chi-town." Trevor climbed in. Jazz music played softly over the speakers and starlights in the limo lit the cabin enough to see our silhouettes.

"Sorry, that was a friend of mine working on something for me." He smiled.

"I understand." I reached out to hold his hand.

The evening was amazing, and Trevor made it clear that he was here for me and that he would be there for me. But, he needed and wanted me to be ready and able to reciprocate if I was interested. He let me know that, under no unequivocal terms, he was playing for anything less than keeps, and if that meant he had to wait a lifetime, he would, as he believed the best things in life are worth waiting for.

"Olivia, I need you to hear me." He turned to me and gently clasped his hands over the sides of my face. "It's not every day you meet someone like you. I've been through my fair share of relationships gone badly, and you know when I met you in Chicago the last thing I wanted was another relationship. Then I met you and you were pregnant with another man's child, but I remember as early as that first hello that there was something so compelling about you that I had to see you again. I think you felt it too." Trevor paused, as he lifted my chin to look at him. "And again, and again, and I just keep thinking about you; how I want to take care of you, be there for you and protect you in any way you would allow me, with every ounce of my being. Do you hear what I am saying?"

"I do," I whispered. Trevor was pouring his heart out and I felt him. It was the first time I wanted to keep listening to a man.

"I'm not asking you to marry me, but I am telling you I love you and I want to be in your life the rest of mine."

I started to cry, burying my face in his chest. "I love you, too, T. I love you."

"Then why are you crying? He lifted my chin to face him.

"I'm so happy and I just wish I was all you are to me." I sniffled.

"Did you hear me? You are more!" He stroked my hair from my face. "Shhhhh. I got you." He pulled me close.

We had always conversed about relationships, our expectations and about being whole when dating rather than fractions looking for something or someone to complete us without much complication. The moments of silence were as comfortable when we just needed to share each other's space, as if engaging in the best conversation.

I shared more into the evening with Trevor about my ongoing legal nightmares and we both decided we'd both get some things in order, as he planned his move to Charlotte. We would be there for one another for support and encouragement in the process. While in Chicago, Trevor was my rock and took me away from the miserable situation I was in and, though I didn't know if or when I would see him again, when I left the city, Trevor gave me hope where it was waning and strength to move on to live my story and rise above it all. Trevor's presence in my life and the timing happened for a reason and most faithfully now, it was happening for a lifetime.

"Trevor, I'm getting paranoid and feel some days like I'm being followed," I revealed.

"You probably are just getting paranoid with this court process. I know it is mentally draining," he offered casually seemingly unaffected.

"You're probably right." We relaxed under the moonlight. "Penny for your thoughts?" I nudged Trevor, as he gazed at the horizon; looking up at the stars as our table service was being set up on the patio. Trevor reached out to hug me closer on the hammock, as he pointed to the stars. The evening was not too warm and not too cool and the outdoor fire pits added just enough lighting to the perfect set.

"I was just thinking that this is the perfect evening. You are more than I could ever pray for, baby girl. Wish upon a star with me," Trevor whispered in my ear.

I cuddled closer under his arm under the moonlight. "I have all my wishes right here and my Jordan. I miss him." I looked in his eyes, resting my chin on his chest.

"I know you do. Olivia, there are a lot of people that find themselves in insane situations just like you and me have, but the choice is ours to let it either wear us down and wear us out or we can take back our lives now and be better than before. Not because we have something to prove, but because we have each other." Trevor spoke gently, as he stroked my hair.

"You're right! And I am going to be all I can for Jordan as a mom and you as your lady."

"I'm sure he gives you the power every day to keep going. Listen to me though. I'm not going anywhere, I can only imagine what you have been through and will go through for the next eighteen years of your life with this character, and I can only suspect it's that much harder with a child, and the courts don't seem like they're helping you. You have to do whatever you have to do to keep your child safe and his well being intact. Anything less would be irresponsible. And, I'll do whatever I can and whatever you need me to do to help you with that." Trevor spoke with sincere love.

"It's second nature to me now that I'm a mom." I gently rested my head on Trevor's chest, stretched out beside him on the hammock. "Just never thought this would happen to me."

"No one could make up this stuff. Baby, we're in this together and I feel you're hurt with Jordan. I do!" Trevor paused as he put his hand on my chin lifting my head to look at him again.

"Maybe not as much as you because you are his mom, but I know Jordan's an amazing child because YOU are an amazing woman! I love you and what hurts you, hurts me."

"Thank you for loving me and for being you and for being in my life. I love you, too, sweetie." The words flowed so naturally. We lingered, as we enjoyed the jazz streaming from the lounge area to the outdoor patio. Men and women mingled, couples embraced under the soft warmth of the fire pits as they warmed the cool night air.

"This hammock feels good, but if you are ready to go do a little dancing, I'm down if you are!" Trevor poked me on my ribs.

"I am good right here!" I giggled. I just wanted to stay in our warm cuddle and feel me enveloped in his body.

"I was hoping you'd say that. I can stay here until the sun comes up, but they'd probably kick us out." Trevor chuckled. "I like this spot. It's cool. Good energy and it's the perfect night for a November eve."

"It has a nice vibe and the crowd is usually mature, which is why I like it."

"And I have the most beautiful girl in the world beside me." Trevor kissed my forehead.

"And don't forget the great wine," I said sarcastically.

"Of course, we can't forget the wine I had flown in from Napa for you!" He chuckled. "You haven't drunk much tonight though."

"Who needs wine when I have you?" I lifted my head to look at Trevor smiling.

We enjoyed the eve another hour relaxing on the hammock, nibbling on the oh so wonderful sweet and salty something mix, sipping on our wine with an occasional dance or two when a song came on that we couldn't sit still to or when I just wanted to shimmy beside the hammock while Trevor admired on.

I was getting more relaxed, almost sleepy, and the days of sleepless nights had caught up to me. "I don't have a hammock, but we can relax on my patio under the moonlight or whatever else you have in mind." I teased.

Trevor gave me a sly smile and without hesitation, ushered the waitress's attention.

"Sorry I'm late. My little guy was sick after a visit with his dear old dad last week and we're just getting back to our routine a week later." I grimaced with a helpless look on my face. I was exhausted, dropping myself down on the couch. But it was my one hour of unrequited time to exhale, leaving lighter than when I came.

"I understand. It doesn't take much for little ones to catch anything and I can only imagine staying wherever he does and not being attentive, it's even easier." She sympathized. "How's he doing now?" Ms. Clara sat in her usual chair beside the window. She gave me some space. She sensed it. I took it.

"He's better now. Thanks! I've become really good at damage control after the visits. It's been a hectic week because I've had to be out of the office most of the week, working from home. This was Jordan's first day back to daycare and I think we both needed some socializing time."

She was reviewing some notes, stopping to look up at me. "Last we visited we discussed your decision to move to Chicago and your pregnancy. Why don't we talk a little about how the both of you interacted before the baby arrived and what more you learned about him during that time?"

"The days were mundane and our interactions were flat. A few weeks after moving in, I ran across Clyde's journals. About a dozen of them."

"Why did you read them?"

"I didn't actually, other than not knowing what they were from the cover and opening them and recognizing handwritten notes. I was just trying to find some room for my things when I was moving in. I just thought it odd and told Clyde I did read them to see what he would say." As I spoke, it was as if something was being loosened from around my neck.

"Why do you say odd?"

"Odd for a grown man to keep journals for more than ten years from some of the dates. He'd been in three or four different cities and two different countries, so these moved everywhere with him."

"Well, you never know, but what did he say when you asked him about them?" She sounded curious. Something inside of me told me she understood. These walls understood everything I was sharing and I felt empowered as I told my story.

"He got very defensive and very suspicious of what I may have read, which was nothing. He said it was his story in case he wasn't around to defend himself and someone tried to lie on him. That is what I thought was odd."

"Wow, doesn't he know that even if he wanted to have his side of the story to discredit another one, he should also realize he'd have to substantiate his story to disprove the other or his story is just hearsay also?" Ms. Clara considered. "What different stories do you suppose?"

"I have no idea and it made me curious to want to read them because his behavior was erratic, but I didn't. That's why I hired the private investigator."

Ms. Clara didn't speak. Although silently, she did. I continued.

"I was suspicious on so many levels. I was having a baby and I needed to know everything about this guy."

"Do you think it was as simple as he was a narcissist and had to write about himself or were you looking to find something to have a way out?"

"Both, but I really didn't want to read them because that would remind me that I made another bad decision. Maybe really bad depending on what I read, and I was having his child and that scared me."

"That was probably a smart decision not to read them. How did you feel when you realized what they were?" Ms. Clara patiently looked at me. *I could make some good decisions, after all,* I thought.

"I was concerned about his past and my health, but my mom always told me if I find myself with the need to check behind someone because I don't trust them, that in itself was all the answers I needed."

"Don't you think the same with the private investigator?"

"I do, but less personal. If he was willing to be out in public then it's no longer personal. It's just straight up cheating, which he was doing in public." I paused to gather my composure.

"Did you decide you were done then?"

"I was done before, but I needed closure to move on and not look back, wondering if I did the right thing. Having a child to think about changed a lot of things." Ms. Clara was nodding her head in agreement.

"What was it like between you two after the baby was born?"

"I just remember counting down the days until we could move and feel free again. Clyde did what he wanted and we did what we wanted. I was learning more about me."

"Like what?"

"Like there was greatness in being still and Jordan inspired me and made me thirst after more every day like a wellspring of hope and faith. He was my rainbow star and he led me to all things new. I realized in the past I either found a way out or ran away, but now, I didn't want to run. I wanted to find myself. I wanted to be happy." I smiled reflectively.

"It sounds like you connected well with your baby and this time was good for both of you. Sounds like you were facing whatever always had you running." Ms. Clara affirmed. "How was Clyde around the baby?" she asked inquisitively, almost as though she knew the answer.

"It seemed that he was jealous of Jordan or maybe he just didn't know what to do with a newborn. I wasn't comfortable leaving him alone with the baby and followed the doctor's advice."

"Your doctor advised you not to leave him alone with the baby? Some people have a real good sixth sense about people, don't they? She may be one of them." Ms. Clara affirmed sitting up straight. "It was a blessing she was your doctor."

"She's from Detroit, so I'm sure she had street sense and she read Clyde perfectly. She thought he was selfish and she didn't trust him after just one visit because he asked questions like, 'How much time and attention does a baby need?'"

"Wow. Really? Do you think he was resentful of the baby?" Her brows wrinkled.

"Definitely, since when I told him I was pregnant and he asked who would spoil him. I think there was hate toward me for changing his life when he wasn't ready and had no control over the choice. I think he also resented that I chose to do it without him because he knew I didn't need him."

"Did he try to bond with Jordan?"

"I guess in the way he knew how, but he didn't spend a lot of time with him. Maybe he just didn't know what to do. I think Jordan sensed it also." I remembered the strained interactions.

"Children have a natural sixth sense because they can't reason and don't have the intellectual capacity, and all they have to go on is their basic instinct and feel a person's energy. They are better at using their intuition than adults are. We lose it because we try to find reason for everything, but we need to use it more and follow our hunches."

"Yes, they are quite amazing little beings." I smiled, thinking of Jordan.

"And research shows that by the age of seven, if a bond is not firmly formed, it can be irreparably broken." She paused. "Even if there is a relationship formed later, there will always be a void," she said gently. "So you shared a baby, a home and basically cohabitated until you decided to move? That had to be hard just living the day to day."

"It was and Clyde made some selfish and irrational requests."

"Like what?" She had a puzzled look on her face.

"He wanted to go to counseling, although he played the victim in the one session I agreed to attend, and he demanded I pump my breast milk at two months," I said, remembering the torment I felt.

"What did counseling do?"

"The counselor fell for Clyde's stories and even suggested I give him time to process having a baby."

"What did you hope to gain from going?"

"Nothing. I really just wanted to keep the peace before I moved," I confessed. "Part of me at least hoped she could shed some light on how we could interact more positively for the baby and co-parent, but I don't think she should have made the unrealistic suggestions she did because it just fueled Clyde to continue behaving the way he did and I didn't stop hearing about it."

"That's a fair statement. But in her defense, some people are good at their game. We'll talk about that more," she said hesitantly. "Did you start pumping at two months when he asked?"

"He demanded it." I was silent. "I just wanted to keep the peace pending our exit." I threw my hands up in the air. I felt cornered. Not by Ms. Clara, but repeating my thoughts and words made me relive the agony. "Jordan was only a few months old at the time and I wanted him to thrive." I felt a lump in my throat, knowing how desperate I felt then.

"I can't believe a father would even suggest such a thing because feeding from a bottle doesn't come natural to an infant as it is and they are just getting the hang of breastfeeding at two months. They need to eat. He could have spent more time doing other things to help you while bonding with the baby in other ways."

"I read the books. He knew I read the books. I told him I read the books. He didn't care or maybe he knew that exactly, so I would purposely have to stop breastfeeding Jordan and we wouldn't be able to bond." I felt helpless as I explained realizing how foolish I sounded. "I hated myself for doing it." I did.

"You were in a tough spot and I know you did what you thought you had to do. What else happened? Go on."

"One day, he locked himself and Jordan in the bedroom, threatening that if Jordan didn't take the bottle then he wouldn't eat. He was crying so hard," I said through my tears.

"I know that must have been hard. We can stop if you prefer."

I shook my head. "No, I need to release my anguish and get beyond this." I took a deep breath. "Clyde has been my kingpin and I have got to move past the anger that has been standing in my way."

"What happened?"

"I threatened to call the police if he didn't let me feed Jordan because he had an arrest with a pending hearing!" I was crying. "That's when I blurted out to him that I hired the private investigator."

"What was he arrested for?" Ms. Clara said shockingly. "You don't have to tell me."

"No, no." I was shaking my head and wanted to continue. "I don't really know, but I know it was after I told him I was moving back to Charlotte and he went out. I don't know what happened, but a police officer knocked on the door the next day to let me know he was arrested. He didn't give details. I didn't ask." I took deep breaths and wiped my eyes with a Kleenex.

"He wouldn't tell you?" Ms. Clara sounded disgusted, as she shook her head.

"No. He said some police beat him up. My attorney is trying to get the records for the trial." My body released the pain that beleaguered me over the past year. I felt lighter as I sat there.

"Did you guys ever discuss your past and if either of you had been molested or abused?"

I was caught off guard with that question. "No, but I did ask who hurt him so bad for him to act the way he did and he said he can't remember."

"What made you ask that?" she prodded. I wanted to ask her the same thing.

"He just seemed angry. All the time. At women. At me. At men. At life. I just wanted some reason." I shrugged my shoulders.

"That's certainly an interesting response that he didn't remember who hurt him because a person usually does, even if subconscious. It could be a cry for help." Ms. Clara thoughtfully paused. "Or a game."

"I'm just so naive."

"It's not naivety. It's just your nature when you give people the benefit of the doubt. They wouldn't have books to write if good and bad things didn't happen to people that we could all learn from. Now that this has happened to you, you know which traits to watch out for and even warn others against. There are many spectrums of conditions that exist and some are more easily identified than others by attitudes and behaviors." Ms. Clara was looking at me for some acknowledgment.

"I just wish I read more of those books that could help me recognize some things to manage it better. There should be a new twenty-first century dating manual." I chuckled nervously. *Maybe I could make good decisions, but this time I was blindsided*, I thought.

"You'd be surprised at the alarming numbers of some of the conditions that exist in our society today listening to the news and hearing how the landscape of our society has changed drastically over the years. There should be more awareness made to people just as there is for health conditions before more pain is caused to so many."

"Why doesn't anyone stop them?" I pleaded, sounding helpless. Stopping them sounded even more helpless knowing now what I had been through and was going through.

"Well, think about it, they are con artists and come across as believable, at least initially, and if and when they are found out, the common thought is to just move on, much like you did, and let someone else deal with the problem. People are so exhausted, having been through similar experiences like yours, that they just want to get on with their own life and save themselves the agony and probably money in the process," Ms. Clara sympathized.

"You're right! After I figured it out and started putting two and two together, all I wanted to do was get away." I was in agreement.

"Things like selfishness, inflated ideas of oneself, lying, cheating and the like is usually enough to want to protect your son. You'd think the courts would take this all into account to protect the best interest of a child, as well."

"Oh, don't get me started on that because I pleaded with the judicial officer for a psychological exam, but she dismissed it and decided to leave it to the judge to determine."

"Didn't you say the court could take up to a year?" She queried with concern.

"Exactly!" I confirmed.

"Heavens! So, until a judge hears, nothing is done even temporarily? That sounds inappropriate because even if there were nothing, I would ascertain that it's better to be cautious than reckless. There are psychological tests people can't maneuver around and most conditions are not as difficult to diagnose as they used to be, as well there are varying degrees of conditions, which could be unhealthy too, where a child is concerned. I know it's got to be hard to wait in the meantime," Ms. Clara empathized.

"I would think they could even do court-appointed screening exams or something of the like, where a child is concerned, and if they don't want to appear biased, they can administer to both parents. I pity anyone that has to deal with a situation like this and it's my hope that the courts will change." I gazed sadly out at the courtyard. It was peaceful. I was too mentally and emotionally exhausted to get worked up.

"Some people's existence feeds at the sacrifice of others' feelings and needs and can also speak to a lack of conscience." She paused. "You've been through a lot and I'll be honest, you have a compelling story."

"Thanks…I think?" I paused, forcing a smile. "If it's okay with you, I'd like to stop for today. I am drained and I really just want to hug Jordan."

"I understand! It's a good time to stop and we can continue on our next visit. Can we do an hour earlier next week?" Ms. Clara checked her calendar as she made a few notes.

"That works," I said in agreement, as I stood.

"You did great today!" Ms. Clara said reassuringly. I smiled warily in return.

We said our good-byes until next time.

As I walked to my car, I processed what Ms. Clara and I talked about. I was beginning to realize that I was of sound mind and good judgment, at least most of the time, but it's neither here nor there when you're up against a sham and when you are not fabricated from the same deceptive clothe.

I noticed I had two missed calls on my cell phone. One was from Walter and the other, Eli.

Twelve
COURAGE

I WAS ANXIOUS, WAITING FOR MS. Clara in the reception area. I needed to quell my worry and nervousness that was building inside me with thoughts that someone was following me and wanted to bring me grave harm.

"Come on back, Olivia." I heard Ms. Clara's voice from down the hall. "Sorry, I was wrapping up on a phone call."

"No problem! Thanks for seeing me." I walked into her office. "I just couldn't wait until Friday and I don't know what to do." I was in panic mode. I was pacing.

"Not a worry, I had someone cancel." She waved her hands. "Please. Sit down. My assistant took your message and said you needed to come in today because you thought you were in danger. What's going on?" Ms. Clara gestured for me to sit in the high-back chair beside her. She had a concerned look on her face.

"I think Clyde has someone following me and he wants to hurt me before the trial. I don't know what to do and I think I should leave town. I don't know what I should do." I looked behind Ms. Clara out the windows, paranoid I'd see someone walking the courtyard.

"Take a deep breath. Let's think about this." Ms. Clara spoke calmly. "First of all, did you talk to the police?"

"Yes, but they said unless I have a description or anyone threatens me directly, they can't do much. I'm not sure if I am overreacting."

"Well, most importantly we need you safe. Did Clyde ever threaten you?"

"Not directly. When I was in Chicago, and we fought a few times, he told me he wasn't responsible for what he'd do to me," I said hurriedly. My leg began nervously tapping.

"Did he ever hit you?"

"He tried to jump on me when I told him about the investigator."

"You told me about that. He had lots to hide and I think that was an act of desperation in the heat of the moment." Ms. Clara nodded. "Does he know anyone here?"

"I never know who Clyde knows, but there is always someone new. If he has so much to hide, maybe that's why he'll try to hurt me. I don't know what to do." I shook my head. I heard my phone vibrate in my purse.

"There is always someone new because people generally figure him out and he moves on." Ms. Clara determined. "I don't think he wants to be a full-time father and he'd be reckless to want to take you out from an emotional or even financial perspective. Being a parent is not easy! You know." She opened her palms to me. "He'd have to know he's the first person everyone would suspect, especially now that the insurance company is on notice also. Did that policy get cancelled yet?"

"No, that's why I am scared!" I exclaimed. "What if he's out of his head and just thinks he can get away with it because he doesn't think of consequences?" I questioned desperately. "I don't think he has a conscience!"

"Breathe. He might be, but we're not going to get into the 'what ifs' or attract these thoughts into our reality. I have to trust that even though the policy is not canceled, they are aware and they have put him on notice as well. We are going to be rational and we are going to trust our instinct and have faith. First and only, God is bigger than him!" She smiled. "Did the private investigator reveal any drug use?"

"No, but he was only able to follow him in public."

"Did you ever tell Clyde everything you knew?"

"No, I just blurted out that there was a PI when he wouldn't give me the baby to feed. He was so mad." I recalled the fight in my mind.

"So he doesn't know what you know or what you don't know, for that matter."

"No. I didn't tell him any details. I think he felt violated because I had him followed."

"Yes. And, because he thought, and probably still thinks, you read his journals. Do you understand why he may feel that way?"

"I had a right to know and he was not being honest with me!" My voice escalated. I was anxious and now irritated.

"I understand." She sounded cautious. "I am asking if you understand why he felt as he did. Violated and angry."

"Yes, but..." I pleaded defensively.

"I'm explaining, so you can understand his heat-of-the-moment reaction rather than true violence. Maybe he has a lot to hide. Does that make sense?"

"Yes." I recoiled quietly. "But people that have lots to hide are the ones that lose it too!"

"Let me say this. You've told me he is very consumed with what people think of him, which is why he tries so hard to get the approval of people. He sounds very self-serving and it's out of the norm to want to carry out such homicidal plans. I am not saying he is not capable and that there is not even a fine line sometimes, but I'm hearing that he likes the mystery of being unpredictable and even erratic and you threatened that. You even controlled it by having a baby when he wasn't ready."

"I just needed to know for my own sake," I said indifferently. I didn't feel any better, but getting it out made me feel stronger, in a sense. At least that someone knew.

"No question. Now tell me what makes you think you are being followed?"

"It seems there is always this black SUV everywhere I am."

"What makes you think they are following you? What type of car is it?"

"A black Escalade. It seems like it's always around, idling or pulling off when I'm leaving a place on my way home."

"That's a fairly common vehicle. Have you ever seen the driver?"

"No, that's just it. The windows are tinted really dark, even the front window, so I can't see anyone."

"Do you know anyone with that type of car?"

"No," I said thoughtfully. I didn't pay much attention to the cars people drove.

"When did you hire the private investigator and when did you tell Clyde about him?"

"I hired the PI when we were still in Chicago and I told Clyde when I confirmed our plans to move back to Charlotte."

"And how long have you been back in Charlotte now?"

"It's been almost a year."

"Okay, so some time has passed and if you wanted to tell anyone about what you knew, he should know you already would have. Did you file in court?"

"Yes, when I found out about the life insurance policy." I was calming down and beginning to think clearer.

"Do you know how long the insurance policy has been in force?"

"The insurance company told me it was purchased after my son was born."

"And when is the court supposed to render its ruling?"

"Not until after the trial next month."

Ms. Clara nodded her head slowly, as she contemplated all the information. "I think you may be worried about court and justifiably the policy and you are allowing your worries and this case to consume you. It has been very frightening, I know. Even though it's disturbing that he got the policy, and how he did, the policy has been in effect over a year and now with everyone watching him, I don't think he'll do anything stupid, even if he has thought about it. To be safe, do you have a friend you can stay with or at least check in with daily until this is done?"

"I talk to my friend Walter every night, sometimes a few times a day."

"Can he stay with you so you can get some rest?"

"He's got kids, but maybe when they are with their mom he can."

"I think you will be okay. I suggested someone to stay with you so you wouldn't worry and you would feel better, not because I think something will happen," she said, encouragingly shaking her head. "Like I said, Clyde would be foolish to do anything with so many people watching him, now or ever. Of course, if anything unusual happens, you definitely need to call the police and make sure it's on record."

"I guess I just didn't think he'd do what he has done and that makes me uncertain about what he is capable of."

"That's smart. Are you scared?"

"Yes." Not to mention the other feelings and emotions I'd been through the past year. I just wanted to get to a place of peace.

"Have you forgiven him?"

"What?" I wasn't following her change of questioning.

"It's important to forgive him and more importantly you."
Ms. Clara spoke gently. "Clearly, you haven't forgotten and you
shouldn't, but I'm not sure if you have forgiven him or yourself
because anger and resentment has you walking in fear, almost as
though you are willing the fear to manifest in your life. Faith and
fear cannot coexist."

"Well, I think it's reckless and irresponsible on my part to
forget the past as a predictor of future behavior, and I don't think
I should forgive and forget what was done and allow myself to
be subject to abuse, especially since the person inflicting it hasn't
shown one iota of guilt or sign of change," I said defensively. I
felt my heart rate rise.

"You are not hearing me." Ms. Clara held her palms out.
"Forgetting is the easy part and I think you'd be a fool if you
did forget, but forgiving yourself is harder because you'll keep
trying to figure out what happened and your anger will keep you
living in a state of fear. Forgiving someone else carries a bigger
element of forgiving yourself also." She looked at me for some
acknowledgement. I nodded hesitantly.

"Clyde just wanted me to just forgive and forget his
indiscretions and his lies and his forgeries like nothing has ever
happened and not be worried about my child." My eyes welled
with tears.

"Of course he does because admitting he did anything would
be harder for him to bear. I wish I could say the end is close, but
you will have to take some time to reconcile the closure in your
mind and you need to give you time also. You've been through,

and you are still going through, a lot, but you're on the right track. You probably second guess your judgment these days, but believe me when I tell you, there are a lot of deceptive people out there and they are really good at what they do. People want to blame themselves, but just know there are some people that do this and they want you to be fearful. Clyde thought you were an easy target, but you stood up to your adversary and that took a lot of courage." Ms. Clara words comforted me.

I smiled, reservedly nodding my head. "Thank you," I whispered. "It makes me feel better to hear that. I used to beat myself up a lot, which is why I came to you, but I'm learning bad things happen to good people. Clyde has been who he is for a long time and may continue to be, but his fate is not my burden."

"Indeed and remember, if people don't have a conscience they are oblivious to how others feel. All you can do is equip yourself to recognize them when they show up and be non-resistant to them to affect you." She paused. "How do you feel now?" She sighed.

"Better." I did. Sometimes just validating my emotions and feelings helped me to feel empowered. I noticed my leg stopped tapping. *I am strong. I truly feel I am.*

"I hope you can feel assured that this is happening for a reason and you need to focus on what that is, instead of dwelling in a place of the past."

I nodded. "I do want to get passed this place."

"I know you do. A lot has happened to you and it's a lot to process. This is a good time to stop. Do you want this to be your visit this week or do you still want to come in Friday?" Ms. Clara uncrossed her legs and sat up straight.

"I think next week should be good." I smiled.

"Claim the victory in court and remember positive affirmations."

"Definitely! I will see you next week. Thanks!" We both stood.

"That a girl! If you need to come in earlier, just call me," she reassured, smiling.

Sweat dripped down my chest, as I felt the sharp, cold, metal edge against my throat. My heart pounded so hard and strong against my chest that I envisioned the little fist-sized organ fighting with every fiber of its being. I focused on its supremacy, wanting same as I struggled to writhe free, though unsuccessfully. I couldn't make out what Clyde was saying beyond the profanities and nor was I interested, as I tried to focus my eyes and scan the kitchen for anything I could get my hands on. My eyes shifted from the cutlery block on the granite counter to the ceramic mug in the sink, until they settled on the cast iron skillet on the stovetop from breakfast. My head was throbbing as I gasped for air. I dug my nails into Clyde's arm that was gripped around my upper body, as I tried to break free from his hold. His skin was hot and smelled, as though he hadn't showered for days and my skin crawled as the stench filled my nostrils. I gagged when beads of sweat dripped off his forehead onto my cheek, as he pinned me against the countertop. Liquid dripped against my collarbone and my finger trailed like a reflex. As I glanced down at my finger and saw the red liquid glisten against my skin, I instinctually shifted to another gear, although everything seemed to be moving in slow motion. I was lightheaded and my body felt weak. I remembered the power of visualization and thought of the story of the mustard seed.

Just at that instant, I thought I heard Jordan's voice call to me from upstairs. "Mommyyy!"

"Stay upstairs, honey…Mommy's coming!" I called out, as my mind caught up to my body, aware that I had to move fast, moving into overdrive. I clenched my fist and braced my arm, struggling to break loose. I slid my body down quickly against Clyde's and thrust my elbow into his crotch with one blow. Clyde let out a deep groan, as his grip around me went limp and his hand, that held the knife against my neck, dropped to grab himself. Clyde was hunched over, gasping for air. As I lunged for the skillet with two hands, I sent the glass pitcher that was sitting on the countertop crashing to the floor in a million pieces. Without a second thought, I felt the cool heavy metal in my palms and took a deep breath. "It's not over until God says it's over."

"How dare you come into my house when I didn't invite you?! This is my life and its not over until God says its over!" I exclaimed, swinging the skillet across Clyde's head, knocking him down, sending him falling to the floor. Bacon grease spewed everywhere. The skillet ricocheted off his head and on to the kitchen floor with a loud crash that shook the floor beneath until it came to a stop. I heaved a sigh of air, as my knees collapsed to the floor. "I'm not done living yet!" I whispered under my breath.

I thought I heard Jordan scream out again, and I was suddenly awakened. I sat straight up in bed as sweat dripped down both sides of my neck onto my breasts; the silk tank I wore nearly soaked. Shaking myself to reality, I quickly realized it was a dream as I assessed my surroundings. Jordan was sleeping soundly beside me, forgetting that I had put him in my bed, so I wouldn't have to wake in the middle of the night. The clock read 12:35 a.m. I must have dozed off.

I thought I heard a car door slam shut followed by an engine start just as quickly. Still dazed from the dream, I wearily rose to double check that the alarm system I had installed last week was engaged from my bedroom keypad. The lights were off and I opened the wooden slat of the blind to look outside, though I couldn't make out the car beyond seeing one turn out of the cul-de-sac in the darkness. I tucked myself under the warm covers and tried to settle back to sleep, or at least a conscious slumber, though I was unable to quiet my thoughts.

Since finding out Clyde had forged my signature to secure a million-dollar insurance policy on my life, a good night's sleep was no longer my reality. As I lay in bed, I was thankful where my life had taken me, knowing it had all been with a purpose. I leaned over and kissed Jordan on his forehead.

Dear Journal,

I'm not sure how I got here, but I believe I'm being shaped for something and this is happening for a reason, although I wished I knew what that was! I am grateful for the blessing of having a child, but I am scared and I've never had to fight this hard. Maybe I should have been clearer when I asked for patience, but this wasn't quite what I had in mind. I know I'm not perfect, but I graciously ask your forgiveness for anything that is displeasing to you and I need you now more than ever. I am strong and I can do this!

Give me strength, give me peace and give me courage!
With All That I Am,
Olivia

When I wrote that journal entry more than two years ago, I had no idea I'd be fighting in the court system to protect the one thing I loved more than life itself. Throughout the unthinkable deception I had lived, I was being continually reminded that everything happens for a reason; the universe knew it and my soul knew it, too, even if I had forgotten. I learned you fight for what is most important to you, beyond principalities and beyond common sense. Principle, I was learning, has nothing to do with the court system, and common sense has even less, especially when the party you are dealing with has neither.

Today was the long-awaited court day for a three-month relationship gone badly. As I got ready that morning, while Jordan was sleeping, so many thoughts bombarded my mind and overwhelmed me. I felt as though I was in a daze and it was all surreal.

The long, drawn-out legal process had been a costly and grueling ordeal, but no matter how hot the flames burned, I shed each layer just as an insect molts their skin for renewal… more resilient and stronger than before. The constant emotional struggle and making sense of this brief, nonsensical liaison left me, most days, desperate for rest and anguished in endless tears that dried my eyes until there was nothing left, except the salt residue. Not even so much as a broken heart or any form of love loss, but plenty of sleepless nights, weight loss and headaches to bear just the same. I felt proud of the image staring back at me in the mirror, as I put my makeup on and noticed every faint character line that defined me along my journey.

I had lived my life learning and trusting each day brought a new experience, a new perspective or just a new day to be lived. Today was no different. I believed in karma and treating people the way you wanted to be treated and, for the most part, assumed most people were good at their core, although ever since meeting Clyde I was questioning those beliefs.

Integrity and being good for my word were the two most important things that defined me; naturally looking for these same things in my associations with people. The course I'd traveled was not without a deliberate perseverance and persistence to navigate obstacles and face challenges head on; some perceivably insurmountable, but I was determined to stay the course, at times even welcomed the opportunity. I felt more empowered and independent pursuing them, as if quenching my thirst, though my current situation felt more like a near drowning. I knew that one day the purpose for this entire ordeal would become blaringly obvious, just as hindsight had been revealed to me before. Hindsight that wouldn't exist if there weren't some sort of understanding that needed to take place, in retrospect, of a person or an experience of its purpose to regain sight that was apparently lost. It did! I had! There is blessing in hindsight!

Mine arrived almost ten months later to the day, after seeing plus signs staring at me like a deer in headlights, to make my next move. Jordan, my blessed baby boy, was the reason I was here and it was in that single moment he was born that I learned, life is about the moments that take your breath away. He had most certainly taken mine.

Sitting on the edge of my bed, I slowly raised my foot to my hands holding my pantyhose and feeling a sense of strength and femininity. I chose a crimson silk blouse and black Emmanuel skirt suit appropriate to the mood for the day. I styled my hair in a single slicked back ponytail and added a brush of lip gloss.

I wanted peace, I wanted closure, and I wanted so desperately to put this part of my life behind me, though I couldn't fathom what the next sixteen years of co-parenting looked like.

I struggled to hold it together and remain calm, as my attorney and I reviewed our notes while we waited for the judge. The courtroom felt cold and congested with walls smeared with emotions of anger, hatred, bitterness, revenge, sadness and joy. Life itself felt stifled inside the courtroom, though I knew today, in this same courtroom, was the first day of the rest of my life.

It had taken every bit of almost two exhausting years, and then some, to get to court to tell my side of the story. With the numbing realization of having a forty-thousand–dollar, and growing, legal nightmare to show for it, not to mention the ongoing counseling therapy, Though I came to appreciate my visits for bringing me one-step closer to closure.

Clyde's attorney casually acknowledged his presence, as she sorted through papers with little conversation and seemed, at best, embarrassed that she represented him. She appeared as though she wanted to get this day over and done with and release her client, hoping not to jeopardize her professional reputation with the judge. She appeared very calm, as she sat expressionless with her hair pulled away from her face, revealing her pale skin.

"All rise!" the tall, stocky, female bailiff announced as the judge entered the courtroom. In dead silence, everyone rose on queue. "The Honorable Judge Bell presiding." Her voice resonated. I felt her confidence.

The judge entered the courtroom from a side door, with a calm and purposeful stride. She was a middle-aged Caucasian woman with a very neatly cropped, short hairstyle, her facial lines very defined and strong. She was almost silver–haired, although some chestnut brown remnants of her natural hair remained. She looked very distinguished. She turned to look at my attorney and Clyde's with acknowledgment, as well as each of us with a look that spoke louder than mere observation. I sensed determination in her gaze.

"Please be seated. The court will come to order," the judge announced, as she readjusted her eyeglasses on the bridge of her nose and sorted through a few papers. "Walters versus Thompson Case. Is this just a legitimation and visitation case with no dissolution of assets? I'm just trying to get my mind around how long this may take. I have a hearing at two o'clock also, but sounds like we should be wrapped up or at least we can start and see how far we get." The judge spoke with candor, or perhaps it was focus, from experience, I assumed.

Clyde was called to the stand first. He appeared brazen as usual, as he walked nonchalantly toward the stand, dragging his feet. His shoulders were slumped and his suit hung loosely with uneven hems. His unshaven face added pounds to his already thick frame and his ashy skin added years to his forty. He paused to look around the courtroom, as if waiting for admiration or applause. There was none.

"Raise your right hand," the bailiff instructed. I noticed a ring on Clyde's wedding finger, as he held up his right hand, his clear, buffed fingernails almost shining. "Do you swear to tell the whole truth and nothing but the truth?" the bailiff asked straight-faced, almost cynically.

"Yes, I do," Clyde responded mechanically. He took the oath of honesty, but it was nothing more than procedure for him. As I observed him, I felt the same indifference as when I met him, wondering how I ever got involved with a man like him.

The subtle contradictions were now blatantly clear to me as I recognized the mannerisms that branded him to his persona.

Clyde's attorney proceeded to paint a beautiful picture of a wonderful person and remarkable father that was denied and robbed of the opportunity to be with his child. Although that picture was a lot less than accurate and devoid of any substantiation, except for a few colorful photographs, it was all they had given whom they were working with. Clyde smugly stared at me, as he gave his testimony, almost tauntingly.

Anxious to do her cross-examination, my attorney scribbled on a pad of paper and passed it to me. It read: *Every dog has his day. Let him have his last!* I smiled, though there was nothing comforting about the courtroom.

Debra, my attorney, was referred to me by a mutual attorney friend. She came with the high commendation of being thorough, professional and tough. She was all that, not to mention compassionate and supportive, being a mother herself. Leading up to the court proceedings, she had told me in all her twenty-four years of practicing, she had never dealt with or met a guy like Clyde. It reminded me of the capriciousness in landing myself here, but it still didn't make me feel any better.

I smiled, as I sat up and straightened my suit jacket and suit collar, as my attorney stood to approach the bench. Her hair was styled off the shoulder in a tasteful bob that accentuated her pronounced jaw line. Her stylish brown suit highlighted her mocha brown skin. She was poised and deliberate, as she stood and looked Clyde directly in the eye, just as a predator does before they pounce on its prey.

"Hi, Mr. Walters. My name is Debra Williams. How are you today?"

"I've been better!" Clyde licked his lips.

"Sorry to hear that." Debra paused momentarily. "Mr. Walters, would you call yourself a liar?" *She got right to the point*, I thought.

"No!" Clyde replied, seemingly insulted by the look on his face.

"I'd like to present to the court Defendant's Exhibit 1, which is an email Mr. Walters sent to my client, confirming you told her that you had a history of mental illness in your family, in an attempt to make her terminate her pregnancy. Do you recall sending that email to Ms. Thompson?"

"If you say so," Clyde responded, mockingly.

"Either you did or you didn't? Please answer the question?"

"Yes, I did that, but—"

"Thank you, Mr. Walters." Debra cut him off. "Mr. Walters did you also answer in your Interrogatories that you or anyone you are related to doesn't have any mental illness?" My attorney was all over Clyde.

"Yes, because I don't." Clyde sighed.

"Well, now I'm confused!" Debra exclaimed, with an exaggerated puzzled look on her face and shaking her head. "Is there a history of mental illness or isn't there because both times it's in writing?"

"There is no history. I made that up!" Clyde stammered.

I noticed the bailiff mouth something into the intercom piece that rested on her shoulder, as she walked with a deliberate, but unhurried, stride beside the stand where Clyde sat.

"Mr. Walters, would you call yourself a liar?" Debra resumed calmly.

"No!"

"I'd like to present to the court Defendant's Exhibit 2, which is another email you sent to my client referencing that you had a child that died at five months old from multiple end organ failure that you further indicated was highly hereditary, again asking my client to terminate her pregnancy," Debra said adamantly. "In fact, you also showed my client a death certificate for this poor child. Mr. Walters, do you recall that?"

"Yes, I did that." He was shamelessly devoid of expression.

"Mr. Walters, isn't it true that, that child didn't exist and you subsequently stated in the Interrogatory questions that 'you didn't have any other children,' other than the child you and my client share?"

"Yes, correct." Clyde cleared his throat.

"And did you explain, in another of your answers to our Interrogatory questions, that you, in fact, fabricated that death certificate that you showed my client for this alleged child?" Debra held a baffled look on her face. There was silence in the courtroom.

Another bailiff entered from the side door, careful not to distract attention from the proceedings and took position to the left of the judge's bench. He was a tall, medium frame man that stood with a look of determination; his eyes focused on Clyde.

"Yes." Clyde glared at me wide-eyed.

"And the Interrogatories were completed as part of this court process, more than two years after initially telling my client and almost two years after your child was born?"

"Whatever your timing is. That's probably correct." Clyde dismissively waved his hands in the air.

The judge removed her glasses, with a look of concern or maybe it was a look of revulsion. I wasn't sure, but nonetheless a blind person could see it. Even a deaf person would be spooked out by the silence.

"Mr. Walters, did you also share this history with Olivia Thompson's obstetrician, who because of this history advised her to do further and more costly diagnostic tests during her pregnancy?" Debra straightened her suit collar calmly, as she returned to the table to read some notes.

"Olivia was determined to have this child," Clyde said heatedly, stroking his forehead with his hand.

"Was this supposed to make her 'undetermined'?" Debra asked sarcastically, unaffected by Clyde's comment.

"It didn't." Clyde scoffed. Clyde's attorney cleared her throat.

"And did you also share that same history with your son's pediatrician after he was born, which to this day makes part of your son's family history in his health record?"

"I don't know what's in his health record." Clyde licked his lips.

"Did you share this history with your son's pediatrician?" Debra redirected.

"Yes."

"If you allegedly don't have these conditions, why would you risk labeling your son like this?" Debra scolded momentarily, losing her own composure.

"Objection!" Clyde's attorney rose from her seat. "There is no basis of any 'labels' as counsel presents!" she stated, making quotation marks in the air.

"I disagree, Your Honor. Mental illness can be a very real condition with very real labels that go with it, and can have some serious implications in the school system with regard to development and academics," Debra argued.

"Sustained. Answer the question, Mr. Walters." The judge looked at Clyde expressionless.

"I didn't want to have a child with Olivia."

My attorney gallantly turned to approach the bench. "I submit Defendant's Exhibit 3 and Exhibit 4. The obstetrician's record and the pediatric record, respectively. You maintained those lies even after the child was born, and did, in fact, have a child with my client?" Debra skillfully concluded, turning away as she gained her composure. "Mr. Walters, would you call yourself a liar?" Debra spoke calmly, as she transitioned smoothly, resuming her line of questioning, once again turning to face Clyde with purpose.

"No! How many times do I have to answer that question?" Clyde clasped his hands together behind his head. He was so far deep in his lies and spoke without a conscience that he couldn't see where my attorney was leading. The male bailiff shook his head, looking at the floor in an attempt to conceal his disapproval. He glanced at me with sympathy.

"Mr. Walters, do you recognize this document?" Debra placed a document in front of Clyde. "This is Exhibit Number 5 for the court." Debra glanced at the judge. The judge nodded with approval.

"It looks like some sort of application," Clyde replied assertively, licking his lips again. "May I get some water?" I was sure with the pressure he should have been feeling he needed more like a waterfall. The judge passed him a water bottle.

"Mr. Walters, can you read the bold captioned title at the top of that application?"

"It says 'Application for Life Insurance'."

"And can you tell me the company logo on that application for life insurance?"

"Freedom Insurance Company."

"Mr. Walters, do you have a friend that works at Freedom Life Insurance?"

"Yes." Clyde shrugged his shoulders and rolled his eyes.

"Have you ever seen that application?"

"Yes, when Olivia and I purchased life insurance policies after my son was born." "Mr. Walters, did you forge my client's signature on that application to obtain a million-dollar life insurance policy on her life?" Debra positioned herself directly in front of Clyde, as she looked at him squarely in the eyes. Clyde was seemingly growing restless on the stand, as he fidgeted perhaps to find a more comfortable position. Under these circumstances, comfort was a relative term.

"Objection! Hearsay." Clyde's attorney stood up, hopelessly trying to save her client from his self-inflicted abyss.

"Sustained. I'll allow. Answer the question," The judge responded as quickly as the objection was given, as if agitated for being interrupted from a good book.

"I don't know who did that?" Clyde said defensively.

The male bailiff gingerly moved closer toward the witness stand, now almost positioned in front of the judge's bench, as he made eye contact with the female bailiff. She nodded in confirmation.

"Mr. Walters, is that your home address on the application, and if not, do you recognize the address?" Debra was clearly trying to hurry Clyde's denial along.

"That's my post office box address."

"Mr. Walters, does Olivia know your post office box address?"

"I have no idea what Olivia knows. She claims to know everything." Clyde snickered mockingly, though no one shared his thoughts. I noticed the female bailiff shaking her head, as I dazed into space. I wanted to be so many places other than this courtroom and my mind wandered to running as it often did for peace.

"Mr. Walters, have you ever had your identity stolen?"

"No."

"Mr. Walters, has my client ever received mail at your post office box?" Debra glanced back at me.

"No!" Clyde exclaimed, growing visibly frustrated, as he threw up his hands.

"Where is this going?"

Although Clyde had repeatedly denied he forged my signature, my self-proclaimed 'pit bull' attorney pursued with the Insurance Commissioner of Illinois and was able to subpoena the original application that blatantly revealed a terrible and poor attempt of a forgery of my signature, including general questions such as income, net worth and place of birth that were also incorrectly answered. I guess Clyde never thought the application would be produced in court and, in the least, that I would pursue, but he should have at least attempted to complete the application as accurately as possible if he was trying to run a scam.

My mind was numb, as I sat listening, unbelieving this all happened and that this had become my life. Clyde's boldness gave me goose bumps, reliving the wicked truth, as he admitted to his evil doings; the truth I was enraged to learn about only in these proceedings and still wondered if things were as he represented now. Clyde spoke callously and premeditated and without any scruples of any wrongdoing. Clyde was convincing that he had no remorse or comprehension of why and how his lies affected anyone, as he sat on the witness stand with a brute, expressionless stare. The more I learned about Clyde over the past few years, the more pity I felt for him, despite everything he had put me through, as I began to realize he was oblivious to the hell he was living; or maybe he was very aware, which made me all the more concerned. I knew for me to try to make sense of someone else's pathology was pointless and I just wanted to steer clear from him.

The judge appeared to be equally appalled with what she had heard given her furrowed brow expressions, as she raised her head to look at Clyde several times during his testimony for any outward signs of guilt or repentance; all to no avail, except for a cold faced gaze in return. I trusted he wasn't fooling her given she had been on the bench some nineteen years and practiced another fifteen prior, as my Google research revealed.

Debra questioned Clyde thirty or so minutes longer, providing more of the same documents, affidavits and derogatory emails of things Clyde had done, said or admitted to, including an arrest. An arrest Clyde paid large sums of money to seal. However, what he didn't realize was that while the records may have been sealed in the municipal state courts, a record is never sealed or expunged from the Supreme Court, not for any amount of money. Clyde failed to realize I was here fighting to protect my child and would do whatever I had to, including retrieving the records I knew existed. Clearly, Clyde's University of Pennsylvania education dollars was not spent on studying a minor in common sense to substantiate his lies and cover the mile long paper trail he left behind. Dealing with Clyde, I was learning to assume everything he did or said was a lie and to work backwards from there. Hindsight was priceless and, in my case, also expensive.

The document count totaled sixteen, including a couple emails where Clyde made derogatory references about me or copied me on emails to his so-called 'circle of friends' under the guise of needing prayer and guidance with an underlying tone that I was an evil person that abandoned him and stole his child. The emails were telling of Clyde's own contradiction; from the selection of people he chose to send it to and the manner in which he littered the email with insults and praises directed at the addressees, including myself, yet claiming himself to be a man that was trying and, even more offensive to me, claiming to be a man of God.

At what appeared to be the end of my attorney's questioning, Clyde turned to the judge to speak. "Judge, I'd also like to ask you something that hasn't been addressed."

"This is out of normal process, but I'll allow because I'd like to hear what it is you have to say," the judge responded in a tone of condescension, as she removed her glasses to look at Clyde.

"In the event that Jordan receives any money or contracts, I'd like to have a trust fund set up in his name wherein I would have access to his money, as well as his mother," Clyde said without hesitation and with as sincere a manufactured face I had ever witnessed to cross his.

My mouth dropped open from what I couldn't believe I'd just heard. Reflex caused me to cover my mouth with my hand. Out of the corner of my eye, I noticed Clyde's counsel cradle her head in her hand in what was obviously non-belief and disgust. It was painfully clear to me over the past year that Clyde's interests were more consumed with what he could gain for his own sake and angering and spiting me rather than caring about his child. When I thought I had seen it all, I was witnessing Clyde's scorn sink to an all time low level.

The judge looked directly at Clyde, as she put on her glasses. "Denied!" she exclaimed, with a look of repulsion as though she had just tasted something painfully bitter. She shook her head dismissively, as she turned to my attorney. "Please continue, counselor."

"No further questions, Your Honor." We couldn't have anticipated a better finish, but for Clyde's own offensive and narcissistic outburst. I was still in shock, as I tried to comprehend his blatant and egotistical request. The bailiffs and the court reporter gathered their poise, taking deep breaths after that last comment.

"Okay, I think we've heard enough from Mr. Walters and all the horrifying lies he told and the terrible things he did." The judge was shaking her head. I assumed she had heard such things before. Maybe even some worse. "I want to hear from your client, but how long do we think we need since he's been on the stand almost two hours. I didn't think we'd need this much time given that the couple only dated three months and there is no contesting of paternity and there is no dissolution of assets. There are also two witnesses, though I can't imagine what information they can provide. Do we have enough time or do we need to reset?"

Both attorneys responded in unison with an unequivocal 'no'. Both, I could only assume, wanting to rid this nightmare case from their workload. I was also in agreement. Clyde's counsel also removed the two witnesses from further testimony. I concluded they didn't have much information to provide.

I wasn't an attorney and I had never been through the court process before, but in anything, I've always thought a good offense is important, but a solid defense is paramount, just as my attorney had proven, as she washed all the colors out of their pretty picture on cross examination. A picture may be worth a thousand words, but a forged document is priceless.

I was on the stand for maybe twenty minutes when the judge interrupted, turned to me and requested I also turn to her to have a very candid conversation about why I was here. In that instant, I felt my heart race, as I turned to her sitting up straighter than I thought my back could extend, thinking it would surely snap.

"Everyone lies and we know, just as your attorney succinctly showed us, he's a really bad liar, and he has done some pretty serious things. I get that loud and clear! Sadly, there are a lot of liars out there and that is why we have this court system. First let me say, I completely understand why you are here and I would do what you are doing, sitting where you are sitting and even paying the large amounts of money I can only assume you are paying to ensure the well being of my child, just like you! Sometimes we need reassurance to validate our anguish and I want you to know I understand why you are here." The judge nodded her head in confirmation, offering some consolation. "That said, unfortunately, your energy and finances are now focused on the wrong thing because of what this guy has done and now you want to correct the wrong that has been done to you." She paused. "But I'm not sure how I can do that for you, let alone make any of this go away. What he did is done and it can never be changed. There is something called the law, and I have to follow it and there is no law that says because he's a big liar, he can't see his child. Does that make sense?" The judge looked directly at my soul with wide eyes.

"Yes." Although, my mind was telling me it didn't make sense and liars shouldn't be allowed to be around children because you never know what they'll do. I came to this courtroom to get some clarity about what is right and what is wrong when it comes to a child. It didn't make sense to me. All I could do was listen, as I sat numb on the witness stand. My thoughts went to Trevor. I missed the comfort of his presence.

"There is no law that says because he forged a death certificate, though I'm not really sure how a person even goes about doing that, that he can't see his child." The judge shook her head with disbelief. "There is not even a law that says if a person has an arrest, he can't see his child! It all comes down to what a person does to the child and if he endangers that child. People can be really great parents, yet completely reckless with their own life." The judge sounded as though she was trying to convince herself. I wasn't convinced and she read my thoughts. "It can happen. Let me say, I am not God, but what I can tell you is, what goes around does come around and you've got to leave the rest to a higher being or this will eat at you and get the best of you and your child needs you well! Let me do my job and give my ruling and you continue to do yours and focus on being the great mom I can tell that you are!" The judge nodded again in confirmation with that same reassurance she spoke about. She turned away to look at the monitor that sat on her bench, as she seemingly was gathering her thoughts.

I affirmed also, with a head nod, holding back the tears that tormented me. If I was reading the distaste on her face correctly, I sensed she felt a little helpless herself and that she indeed wanted to jump from her bench, matrix style, and deliver a good old fashion beating and handle Clyde herself. *Take a number*, I thought. It seemed as though she had already decided what she could and would do within the law, and didn't need to hear more of the exhausting same, but that she had to give the appearance of vetting out all the facts and do so judiciously and prudently before rendering her order. I was speechless as I felt relief just hearing the judge corroborate my feelings, but I still felt helpless.

As I remained on the stand, I resigned to accept that people and life aren't always what I'd expected, and instead focused on the serenity to accept the things I couldn't change then, and more undoubtedly, couldn't change now. A serenity knowing people project their misery out of their own deficiencies and wretchedness, when they realize they have nothing to lose.

Turning again to me, the judge asked, "Do you know his mother and do you think she could tell you more about his health history to make you more comfortable? Or are there some medical records we can get?" The judge looked at my attorney, realizing this would have been an obvious consideration by my attorney. The judge appeared confused. "What do you think?"

I took a moment to ponder her thought. I first considered that she asked me the question because she had reasonable question to ponder herself, so my response would not be something she did not herself contemplate. I wanted to scream that I believed

Clyde was a liar and a narcissist that lived without a conscience and without consideration for others and I didn't know his mother or anyone in his family and that Clyde never told me about his childhood because perhaps there was something to hide, but my better judgment told me to refrain. There was the other more logical aspect to consider to her latter question. Clyde was forty years old and the chances of his pediatrician still practicing or even alive were not necessarily realistic, let alone, if the records still existed. I wasn't interested in chasing those dead end possibilities or the very good possibility of Clyde giving me bogus information and sending my attorney and I on a wild goose chase.

"I don't really know his mother and can't comment on what she could say or not, but given what I've been through, I need to be sure for my child," I said quietly. I declined to express much more, short of my own disgust, leaving it to the judge's discretion, hoping she'd sense my concern and hesitation and be prudent to her own. "I don't know what the truth is and what the lies are anymore because there have been so many, but I came here hoping the court could make sense of it because most days it makes my head spin. I am guilty of having a child with a person I didn't completely know and didn't even trust and wasn't married to, but I chose to give life and it's a decision I can live with, but I digress. I believe your original question was 'What do you think?' and truthfully, I really don't know what to think because of all the lies." My voice cracked and tears began to well in my eyes, as I felt my body go limp under my clothes.

All of a sudden, my suit felt two sizes too big and the pain and agony of the past few years overwhelmed me.

"I do hear what you are saying and everything you have said is reasonable. There is a lot of information to review and I'd like a few days to give consideration to it all." The judge appeared to be in a quandary. "I'd also like to confer with a psychologist as to the mental illnesses that can be diagnosed in adulthood and what, if any, intervention can be done? Do you think that will help make you comfortable with all this and your son's health record?"

"I'm here because I have to defer to you and this court. You've heard most of the facts, but short of having a week trial for a three-month relationship, which would be absolutely insane on so many levels for all of us, I can only do all I can do to protect the well being of my son, whatever it takes. I can only ask that you make your deliberation with everything you have heard and with my child's best interest in mind. Thank you!" My voice diminished to a whisper, as I bowed my head and held back the huge lump in my throat that was now choking me.

I knew my life would change from the moment I saw the 'plus' signs, but the 'changes' I had imagined were in the form of midnight feedings, deprived sleep, potty training, school grades and peer pressure; all of which I was ready to accept as a single mom. I did consider, maybe at worst, Jordan's dad would be a dead beat—inconsistent with his visits or child support and even the unpleasant exchanges you hear about—but I never could have imagined, in my wildest nightmares, the unpredictability and torment of parenting with a person more interested in unleashing his venom at me than caring for an innocent child. Now, I was attempting to make sense of forgeries, falsified documents, deception and grandiose lies to find the truth and settle my concerns.

"Okay, let me do some deliberating because there is a lot to consider here." I snapped out of my thoughts as I listened. "You have to trust in the process! Court is done and I will send my order out to Attorneys Williams and Pawlins in the next few days." The judge slammed her gavel on her bench.

I sat frozen, as I remembered the mantra I had coined when I decided to leave Clyde and leave Chicago, repeating it quietly under my breath, F.T.B.—Faith in my Creator, Trust in the process, and Believe in myself. The judge's statement to 'trust in the process' was my affirmation that God was indeed in the courtroom, as I instantly felt His peace cradle me. I looked over my shoulder to see if He was, in fact, standing behind me. It was surreal and it wouldn't have been the first time I felt God in my presence. I had faith, I had trust, I believed and I knew everything would work according to His plan and that God doesn't close one door without opening another; or at least a window to breathe some fresh air in and, if the fresh air happened to blow in someone like Trevor, then I'd slam the door shut myself! Seriously, I was still standing and I was thankful at least court was over.

The order would be anxiously anticipated and, I knew whatever was decided, I'd have to let it rest and find a way to emerge on the other side with the strength and courage to move forward with wisdom from the experience. The judge's remark that *'she'd pay any amounts of money to do what I was doing'* was victory enough in my mind, and validated my plagued thoughts and feelings of the past two years, as I trudged this path. Although it felt like a huge victory on the inside, I needed the victory on paper also.

Thirteen
TRIUMPH

ON MY WAY TO PICK UP Jordan at daycare, I was looking forward to the weekend. We had nothing planned other than a few errands and maybe a visit to the park. I usually kept the weekends open to catch up on whatever needed catching up on, as well as much needed sleep from a very deprived week. The mental stress and sleepless nights had me exhausted beyond any physical limitation. As I turned into the daycare, my phone rang. My attorney's number came up on caller ID. I immediately picked up.

"Hey, Ms. Debra."

"Hey, lady, I got the final order from the judge. I will scan it in later for you to read in detail, but I can give you the *Reader's Digest* version now, if you want. Is now a good time to talk?"

"Time is as good a time as it's gonna get!" I took a deep breath, feeling my body tense up.

"Okay, here it goes. You got joint legal custody, with final decision-making being yours and no need to confer with him. The judge did order a psychiatric evaluation for Clyde and at his expense. And, the life insurance policy has been canceled. Now, regarding visitation, she did grant overnight visits every three weeks since he's had them without incident, but not the usual two since he lives in Chicago, which I told you he would get since he fought for them, and the judge told you also that she needs to stick to the law. The summer and holiday visitation is also the standard alternating schedule, with minor deviations."

My heart sank immediately, as I temporarily went deaf and didn't hear much else Debra said.

"He also has to pay the healthcare from now on also, which should be a good amount of relief to you. Those are the main points, but you can review it and let me know if you have any questions. I need to inquire within seventy-two hours, which is Monday morning if you do. Okay?"

I attempted to understand what I'd just heard Debra say, momentarily considering the benefits of not being able to hear what my mind couldn't process. Maybe there was bliss with ignorance and in this case, maybe the inability to hear.

"Olivia, are you there? Olivia…"

I snapped back to reality, as a knot formed in my stomach. "I'm sorry. I didn't hear anything passed the point when you said he got overnight visits." I spoke slowly as if I were in a trance. "They think a toddler that is upside down when he returns; screaming in the night for a week is 'without incident'?

The court doesn't think the emotional well being is in the best interest of the child?" My voice escalated.

"Olivia, I told you unless this guy physically abuses Jordan, he'd get standard visitation. The judge told you herself that there are no laws for the things this guy did to you with regards to his rights to see his child." My attorney tried to offer some explanation though my mind couldn't process any, as I sat frozen in the car. Parents were walking into the daycare with happiness to pick up their little ones, completely oblivious to the innocence and value of their being.

"I know, but I thought they'd at least consider what he did. It just doesn't make any sense that my little guy can't tell me what's going on yet. Who knows what else has to happen!" I exclaimed, as I began to cry and thought of Jordan's anxiety after he returned from a visit; the way he clung to me so tight, tossing and turning while he slept. I felt completely helpless. I reached in my console for a tissue.

"You have to be strong and you have to remember Psalm 37 like I told you. *Do not fret because of those who are evil or be envious of those who do wrong; for like the grass they will soon wither, like green plants they will soon die away.* You have to trust that. I've seen it so many times. It will change after the order because their charade with the judge and their family and friends is over. He's still around and being noble. Some of that is for the court and some of that is because he's got to put up the fight and make you look like the bad guy. You didn't give him a choice when you got pregnant and you left him and he's angry.

You know that and I know that, but he should be lucky enough that you are the mother of his child!" Debra offered.

"I've been praying for strength to accept the outcome, but it's just not so easy when it's your child. This is my baby." I shook my head though no one could see my helplessness. "I know I've got to move past this with courage and work on changing the things I can, starting with me and I know I can't change him, but I don't know if I can."

"You have to! That's the wisdom part in this journey; knowing what you can and can't change. He wants to make your life miserable since you made the choice to have the baby without him and he has to make you look like the scorned ex, but don't let him. Keep doing what you're doing and keep being the great mom you are and doing right by Jordan. Jordan is a smart child and he's all that matters." A beep came through on my other line. It was Eli. I wondered what he was calling for.

"I know, but some days it's hard and I guess it just can't come soon enough for me." I acquiesced.

"You're doing everything you can and I am so proud of you for dealing with all of this as well as you have. Clyde will reap what he has sown, but you have got to let this go and let God handle it from here. Trust me," Debra said firmly.

"Thanks. I need to hear this because some days I think I'm losing it. I'll review the order and let you know by tomorrow if I have any questions. What I do know is, at least the insanity of the long court process is over and I am glad for that. I just never could have imagined this would be the reality of my life. It's been an absolute nightmare!"

"No one can because if we could, no one would need faith and hope. Stories are made from tragedy and tribulation and without them, there would be no stories of triumph. You wouldn't be the person you are today—stronger, wiser, and more courageous—if it weren't for this experience and, lady, that beautiful baby boy is yours to remind you every day to stay the course. God chose you because He knew YOU could handle it." Debra paused. "You should think about writing a book. Like a testimony of your faith, so others can be strengthened."

I chuckled. "I think I'll leave it at journaling for now, at least until I'm passed potty training, but you never know." I hesitated. "All things aside, Debra, I have to ask you… do you honestly think we did all we could, given our time in court was cut short? It just seems as though he's getting away with everything." My tone changed to serious.

"Olivia, I do! I know it may feel as though he is getting away with something, but he still has to answer to God. He can think he's fooling some people some of the time, but he won't be able to fool all people all the time and eventually it will all catch up to him and he'll be fooling no one. This is not your battle!" She was adamant. "Your job is enjoying your child and being all you were called to be. Don't get caught up in what Clyde is not doing, when you should be focusing on what you need to do."

"I know and you are so right!" I agreed, nodding my head, as I looked around contemplative. Her words encouraged me.

"You've got to believe that and live it," Debra affirmed.

"Thank you! I'll call or email you in the next day with my questions, if I have any."

"That's all I ask. Do something fun this weekend and give that little guy a hug for me. This was a win, Olivia! Trust me!" Debra paused. "You really should think about writing that book."

"I guess. Thank you always! Talk to you soon." I hung up the phone and wiped my eyes with the tissue. I opened the valet mirror to inspect my face before heading into the daycare. My mood was somber and all I wanted to do was hug my baby.

I was on my way to meet with Eli for an afternoon latte. He called to let me know he was in town on a case he picked up at the last minute and he'd be in town for a few weeks.

I was wearing my Prada sunglasses to hide my red, puffy eyes. My hair was pulled back into a ponytail under a baseball cap. I grabbed a window side table while I waited for Eli. I wondered if people could see the same bewilderedness I felt. My body was exhausted from another sleepless night. As I waited, my thoughts wandered to past relationships that didn't work out for one reason or another, all of which now seemed trivial and premature in their demise compared to this ordeal. I'm not sure why I was so consumed with how I got involved with a character like Clyde, but I desperately wanted to believe it happened for something greater.

Eli entered the café, making a casual glance around, locating my presence. With a head nod acknowledgement, I stood to join him in line to order our drinks after greeting him with a hug.

"You look fantastic. How are you?"

"Thanks, Eli. Still doing damage control, I see. I'm good." I said looking around the café.

"How old is that little guy now?"

"He's twenty-two months old." I raised my eyebrows in wonder.

"Wow. Time flies. And, how's the crazy dad?" Eli asked hesitantly.

"I just got the order yesterday, so, at least, I can move forward and put this behind me." I looked down.

"Hey, what's wrong? Is it the order?" Eli put his arm around my shoulders. "How did it turn out?"

"He still got visits. I just feel so helpless." I wanted to collapse and cry, but I maintained my composure; already paranoid everyone could see through my cover. "If they intended to stick to standard visitation, I don't even know why they didn't just tell us that from day one. Would have saved lots of money and time!"

"That's exactly why! It's a big moneymaking process for the courts. The courts have it backwards, if a person doesn't have to prove their innocence when a child is involved instead of defend their guilt."

"I've given up on the courts," I said dismissively. "They're totally backwards."

"Olivia, I'm so sorry. How have you been holding up?" Eli reached to lift my sunglasses away from my eyes. I shyly closed my eyes and turned my head.

"I'm exhausted and feel like I'm living in a nightmare most days. The courts are just so frustrating and I can't believe they don't err on the side of caution where a child is concerned."

"Well, from what I've heard from you, it's pretty sad the courts don't exercise more vigilance with this character." Eli spoke frankly.

"Sad does not even accurately describe it. I'm thinking more like shameful that a court claims to protect the best interest of the child, but yet allows a person that forged my signature and a death certificate to be around a child, without supervision nonetheless." My voice began to crack.

Eli returned his arm around my shoulders, as we ordered our drinks.

"Wow. What is shameful is that you were able to prove those things to a court and they still gave him visitation."

"Oh and he admitted to the fake death certificate."

"What? That's crazy! And the courts didn't think that someone, who would do it *and* admit to it, has zero conscience or remorse for doing so, has a problem?"

"No and now it's got me all freaked out and now I think someone is following me." The comment itself made me feel paranoid when I said it. I looked over my shoulder and around the café again. We returned to the table with our drinks.

"What makes you think that?" He sounded surprised. Almost animated. "Did you get the life insurance policy canceled?"

"Yes, but it always seems like this car is everywhere I go and it's as if I hear car engines in stereo. It's just unnerving!"

"Well, you're not alone," he said nonchalantly.

"What do you mean, I'm not alone? Is someone following you too?" I was confused.

"No, no, I mean there are probably so many people watching out for you that you are not alone. Like angels are watching over you. Sooner or later it's all going to catch up to him because he can't keep this up and he'll fall off the face of the earth. Eventually, a guy with a rap sheet or a dark past will hurt himself. I've seen it before."

"Well that time can't come soon enough. All of his contention is just more evidence that he's more interested in angering me, than being a parent. I just hope he gets hit with my attorney's fees!" I could feel the anger build up inside me.

"A guy like this has to carry on like the victim. We talked about that," Eli said cynically. "Has he contacted you? When is the next visit?"

"No. Not until next month. It just makes me sick and it's so obvious to me now," I said with disgust. "I don't even like to see his name come across my email."

"Has he threatened you in any way?" Eli questioned anxiously like a cat ready to pounce.

"No, he just litters his emails with derogatory insults and that I'm unstable and need counseling."

"Consider the source. This from a guy who forged a death certificate. Let the record show who is unstable." He chuckled. "You have to document everything with liars."

"That was the first thing I learned dealing with him. I just want to put this behind me and get me back and start living life again."

"You know, when you first came to me, I assumed he was just a cheating guy and I see that all the time, but after some of the things you've told me in our conversations, I realized this guy has bigger issues and has to win and be in control. And, look what he lost?" Eli opened his hands, as he waved them up and down in my direction glancing at me. "He's going to try to make you insane in the process too because then you will look like the scorned one. I know the judge probably has to stick to the law, but hopefully you'll be awarded the fees. You are being watched."

"I guess. I have ten days to write my letter to the judge. Thus the java." I pointed to my cup. I reminded myself it would be a late night after putting Jordan to sleep. The midday coffee was needed. "No amounts of money will ever justify what he has done." I was contemplative. "What do you mean I'm 'being watched'?" I felt my own fear escalate.

"I just mean that the judge and the legal angels are watching over you and hopefully he will have to pay your legal fees." Eli spoke dismissively. The only thing calm about me was the caffeine in my blood.

"Oh. I hope so, too."

"Parenting should be considered a privilege, not a right and a child should have rights to their own future best interests with some direction from the court."

"Let's change the subject. I don't want to talk about this anymore because I don't want to keep rehashing what I can't change!"

"Okay. How are you enjoying Charlotte the second time around?" Eli switched the subject as quickly as I had spoken. He didn't miss a beat. After all, he was a private investigator.

"It's easy here. People are friendly."

"How do you like your townhome?"

The question caught me off guard. "I love the neighborhood, but how do you know I live in a townhome?" My memory had lost me if I told Eli I lived in a townhome. I was searching my mind. I wasn't surprised if I'd forgotten with everything I had been through the last few years.

"You told me when you were moving to Charlotte that you were going to look for a townhome," Eli answered quickly. "I just assumed that's what you ended up finding."

"Well you have a good memory because I don't remember what I do most days immediately after doing it." I shook my head from a fog. "I'd forget my head most days if it weren't attached to my body." I smiled.

"I think that's referred to as baby brain. A good memory is a job requirement for me, so I remember everything!"

"I'm sure! That baby is almost two years old, so I'm not sure how much longer I can claim baby brain anyhow, but I'll take it."

We chatted more about life and contemplated getting together again over the next few weeks. I felt comfortable and safe with

Eli. Other than telling me he was getting together with a family friend and his aunt, he was vague about his work here and his availability. I respected it was personal.

No one prepared me for what would happen in life, but my mom and dad did prepare me to be ready for what might come. My parents gently loved me with every piece of their soul and even though they didn't always shower me with affection or shelter me from pain, there was always a silent assuredness that I mattered and that I was protected. I'd be forever grateful for their understanding. I'm not exactly sure what or how they did it, and I'm not entirely sure they even knew what they did, but they did everything to the best of their ability with the information they had coming across the globe from a foreign upbringing and an arranged marriage in hopes to find a better life for their children. They taught me that if I was willing to learn and be teachable, then I would be equipped with the knowledge to make good decisions and I could most certainly conquer the hardships that came in life. I prayed I possessed enough of whatever it was they had to pass that same wisdom onto Jordan; to persevere and have faith and to have the courage to face the challenges life inevitably would bring.

The more I read and talked to others, the more I learned of the huge numbers of single mothers in our society that are heroically raising children—happy and productive children. I had heard countless stories of conscientious and good-natured children raised by single mothers. It was a road I wouldn't be the first to travel, and certainly not the last, but I felt in some way that if I could pave that road just a little less rocky and fill some of the potholes along the way, another single mom and another child could go down the road with a little less bumps and travel the road to love, happiness and peace. I didn't have all the answers, but I was sure I was on this journey for a greater purpose and I was somehow uniquely chosen to travel this journey.

Throughout life, I was learning that adversity is not about the details of what happened or even the perpetrator that violated you, but more where you find yourself; learning from the lesson when you are standing in the eye of the storm, looking that storm in the eye, emerging on the other side more empowered from the experience. That road from misfortune to victory is sometimes a humbling one, but where faith exists, doubt and fear cannot reside, for that would be in direct contradiction to what faith stands for.

At forty-two, I was learning to conquer fear, hurt, pain, anger and betrayal for the first time in my life and although it was an uphill reality to bear, I held courage as my shield and I was healing from the inside out. I was happy in spite of my circumstances and I was not going to allow Clyde to steal my joy. Unfortunately, for him with every day that passed, I was one more day beyond him and one more day wiser to his predictable and self-serving behaviors.

I worked around the clock with seven more days to complete the letter to the judge for attorney's fees; working nine to five drinking coffee, taking care of Jordan and our home, while writing my letter into the wee hours of the night drinking more coffee, followed by a sluggish morning and doing it all over again the next day. Debra was kind enough to share sample letters to model, as I quickly concluded that the attorney fees letter was more work than I realized and could have alone cost me a few thousand dollars or more just sifting and sorting through everything that had happened in the past year with all the documents and correspondence where Clyde was unreasonable, litigious, contentious and how he basically stone-walled during the proceedings of this case racking up more attorney's fees for us both than were necessary. Clyde acted more often than not representative of this behavior, so it became more a measure of quantifying how much of everyone's time and money he wasted with blatant disregard rather than having to qualify that he did as we succinctly showed he did in the proceedings. He was premeditated with his lies with a malicious intent to deceive and hurt, which spoke for itself to the justification of my pleadings. The courts and the system soaked every penny along the way like a leach that remains stuck, hoping for more.

My fifth and final nine-page draft letter asked for all my attorney's fees in addition to that same amount for the unnecessary Guardian Ad Litem fees Clyde was insistent the court appoint, only adding to the contention.

Two days away from the deadline, I set out the next morning to hand deliver the letter to the judge choosing not to take any chances that snail mail would not arrive in time. The long narrow hallways and walls felt rigid in the silence, as I was humbled at the thought of the forefathers that fought to establish the court system of laws and rules to preserve and maintain order in a chaotic world. All which seemed hypocritical to me now with blatant evidence of the ever-changing times we live in. Completing the letter was a daunting task in itself, but hand delivering it to judge's chambers was empowering on another level as I sensed relief that closure would soon follow.

The Judicial Case Manager to the judge was professional and helpful as she spoke. Her eyes were very focused and her voice direct, as she explained the course of the proceedings while entering some information into her computer. She indicated the judge would deliver her ruling to my attorney within seven days. *Another long awaited seven days,* I thought. *Another seven to the almost two years I have already been in court waiting. I am strong.*

Fourteen
CLOSURE

MANAGING JORDAN'S CHANGES AT THIS POINT were development related, though the days and weeks following his return from sporadic visits with his father brought a new dimension of changes before resuming his regular routine and Jordan being his jovial self again. His father didn't take interest to Jordan's needs and was clueless of the importance of a routine for a young child as their measure of developing trust and comfort with their caregiver. And, although Clyde did things to anger and hurt me, or so he thought, he was only causing irreparable damage to the relationship with his child. I constantly prayed for Jordan's comfort and safety, continuing to fight, with every fiber of my being, for my child. I chose to pray so I wouldn't worry because I learned if I was going to worry there was no need to pray.

Accepting the call to be a mother at the age of forty was the most amazing blessing to me. And, while I recognize having a child at a much younger age could bring it's own challenges from a financial or even emotional standpoint, the fight I found myself in was more than any mother should ever have to endure, at any age.

"So you got the court order?" Ms. Clara anxiously closed the door behind her.

"Yes." I was nonchalant, choosing the high-back chair near the window.

"Are you happy with the outcome?" She hesitated.

"Happy is a relative term. I'll just say I'm glad this part is done, but I have to accept the order as the law and trust my attorney and I did all we could." I was vague. I was broken. I was discouraged.

"So, he got visitation like your attorney advised he would? Are there any parameters, at least?" She sensed my reservation.

"Yes, but nothing out of the ordinary. Just the usual schedule and times and transition emails, but there's no requirement that he has to tell me where he stays, notification requirements or who can pick up the child at least until more information was obtained." I paused. "I just thought based on what he did there would have been some restrictions." I sounded helpless. I felt helpless.

"I can't believe there isn't. Can you tell me what you are feeling?"

"Anger mostly. I have never known anger like this, or maybe everything in the past now just seems trivial in comparison."

"What or who angers you most?"

"Besides all of it?" I held a sarcastic look on my face. "Mostly, I'm angry that Clyde thinks he can get away with all the things he did and that he didn't think it would catch up to him, but I'm also angry at the court system because he was able to. And, the judicial advocate had the nerve to tell me to exercise common sense!" I stood up and began pacing. "I mean, common sense wouldn't have me in a court paying all this money if I didn't have to!"

"What was that about?" Ms. Clara asked defensively.

"I asked her how she suggested I exercise common sense when I receive derogatory emails from someone who produced a fake death certificate and had my signature forged. This is clearly not common sense or doing the right thing. When is it the damn court's responsibility to exercise some common sense in all this where a child is concerned, is what I asked her."

"And what did she say?" Ms. Clara looked sympathetic. I knew she felt my fury as a mother.

"What could she say? Nothing!"

"I know it's frustrating, but they did give good indication early on that they may not. Would you agree?"

"Well, yes from the judicial advocate, but I thought at least the judge would exercise some reasonable legal jurisdiction."

"This may be the sad reality of the state of our legal system and current laws. We've already decided that this is bigger than

Clyde and this may even be bigger than the legal system, or at least that may be how we have to look at it."

"I guess, but that is concerning since there are so many children out there and the divorce rate keeps getting higher. It's stressful enough being a mother as it is, but to have to fight these fights without a court that is supposed to protect at least your child is just disconcerting."

"I agree, but you have to forgive the courts too if you want to move forward. If you stay here, it will cripple you and prevent you from fulfilling your destiny. What else can you do unless you appeal the court's ruling?"

"And spend more money. Nothing. It's hopeless." It felt hopeless. I paused. "Let me just say I understand how people lose it, but I am thankful I am not that person and that I know God, but I do understand how it can happen, especially when you have a child." I stared out the window, holding back my tears.

"Besides granting visitation, do you think the courts could have done more?"

"Absolutely!" I exclaimed. "First of all, the legal action proceeded at a snail's pace while my child was caught in the system. The court appointed a Guardian Ad Litem who served little to no purpose just trying to build her resume freshly out of law school. I don't know if they have to do any child psychology studies, but the same court put out a guide of healthy visitation parameters for children, that they didn't even follow themselves. The Guardian didn't even have any children and served absolutely zero purpose." I resumed my pacing, sensing my fury growing once again. I needed to get a hold of myself. *I am strong.*

"Really? That should almost be a requirement. Seems if a person who is an advocate for children should at least have to have one or at least have studied about them and their well-being." Ms. Clara supported. "She probably lacks the experience and insight necessary to consider the psychological and emotional needs of children."

"It just seems that the system is not set up to protect the best interest of the child because everyone is too busy trying to remain objective and get paid. I understand not taking sides, but someone has to be the voice for the child since they don't have one." I resumed my seat, feeling exhausted though it was more emotional than physical.

"I agree. You bring up some very valid points and being a parent does changes your entire perspective. You should consider filing an appeal or when he goes against the order, you file him in contempt."

"Where will that get me?" I threw my hands in the air. "What he's already done is cost me ridiculous thousands of dollars and landed me where it would have been if I did nothing. In the least, I think the standards of the court system should be seasoned to the theatrics of the many characters that present, not to mention where any seed of doubt existed or debauchery, and should be intolerable of such. I think court systems should be the legislating institution since it's the very premise they were founded on; to bring justice when justice comes undone, but that is just one mother's opinion."

Ms. Clara was nodding her head in agreement. "Probably many. Did the life insurance policy get cancelled?"

"Yes, finally! Thank God, but only after I paid a lot of money to prove that forgery too, after Clyde continued to deny it! He should have been arrested for that alone!"

"You know forgery is a criminal offense and the statute of limitations varies, but that's one more thing to pursue. Are you up for that also?"

"No. It's not my battle. He'll get what he has coming to him because that's the law of karma. I believe in that! If he wants to keep trying me however, I just might," I said with a blank stare. I hadn't ever known vengeance and didn't even want to own that statement.

"I'm not sure he's not already getting some of what he'll have coming to him, but some people believe they are above everyone, including the law. He'll cross the wrong person eventually. You have the right attitude that this is not your battle because you have that beautiful child to focus on."

"I'm just disgusted because I didn't even know about all these lies until we were in court, after my child was born! It's almost two years later, so Clyde definitely had malicious intent since he found out I was pregnant because he never came clean or came to me claiming to have a change of heart. If in fact, he ever did. I think if this guy is capable of doing *any* of the things we proved, we can't say what he will and won't do with a child with any certainty."

"I think that's a reasonable consideration, but unfortunately it sounds like that's not the way it is. I can only imagine how agonizing this is for you every time your child has to go on a visit. I believe if you get to a place where you can be unemotional towards Clyde, he will fall away on his own or at least the anxiety will lessen for you because you will not be in that place. He would be a fool to do anything less than what the order specifies at this point, and focus on being a good father. There are too many people watching him and he should know you would go back to court by now. How often are the visits set up for?"

"He requested every three weeks."

"They're trying to foster a parent-child relationship and give him a chance to redeem himself. It's usually only two nights and that's if he keeps all his visits since you said he already cancels a lot and that was when he had to make a good impression to the court."

"I get it, but my child is still young. I do believe children stand to gain from being raised with the balance of a mother and a father, but we're living different times now and I don't believe the child's wellbeing is in any way compromised when they're raised in a single parent home with love and peace. A parent's mental suitability and stability should speak for more than chromosomes."

"I believe in certain situations that's true and sometimes it's more unhealthy for a child to witness a dysfunctional relationship or a person than a single parenting situation. Most of the research out there reflects when a single parent home is below the poverty line or the parents are uneducated, and there may be issues, but otherwise the outcomes of the children have shown the same or more successful and balanced from a healthy loving single parenting situation."

"We proved one parent was arrested." I grimaced.

"Yes and you got custody. His time amounts to less than ten percent of Jordan's time. He's not having much of an impact other than knowing he is his father, which will be good for him to know his father. I think now that the order has been rendered, you have to find true closure. You have to start living now and let all your blessings come to you. Now is the appointed time to put this all behind you." Ms. Clara's voice was quiet. Like a spirit was speaking to me and opening my soul. "You did the right thing by allowing him the opportunity to witness his child's birth especially since that is what he claimed to want. You had no way of knowing any of this would happen or that he wasn't who he said he was." She paused. "Do you have any regrets?"

"Yes and no. Yes, because it's been a costly and arduous process while I was pregnant, but no, because I have the sweetest present in all of this. I did hit the jackpot! I never would have known this and I'm glad I found out sooner than later." I pulled my hair back from my face, and stretched my legs in front of me. I felt more relaxed. More free. Like a weight had just been lifted simply making the statement. I meant it.

"I agree. You needed to know. Do you still feel scared?"

"No, I'm better there too and I check in with my family and my friend Walter daily. It's a little surreal because I do feel like I am being watched."

"You are. In a good way. You give power to your thoughts and your words." Ms. Clara paused to look at me for any acknowledgment that I followed her thoughts. "That's true faith."

"I understand." I nodded. "I feel like closure will come next now since court is over. That was a big deal for me."

Ms. Clara was nodding. "Now, let's infuse our being with positive affirmations. Reading them and living them daily."

"I have a mantra I coined when I was pregnant," I said optimistically.

"That's a great start! Can I ask you what it is?"

"F.T.B. 'F' is for faith in my Creator, 'T' is to trust in the process and 'B' is for believing in myself." I sat up straight, feeling empowered just speaking the words.

"I like that! It's powerful and we need to put that out in the universe and breathe it until it becomes your way of living." Ms. Clara contemplated. "Be aware of what you allow yourself to think about and always determine if your thoughts are from a place of fear or a place of faith."

I smiled. There was silence as we stayed in that moment.

"It sounds like you were methodical and planned out pretty much from the day you met him, to when you found out you were pregnant, up until when you decided to move to Chicago and then back to Charlotte. Truthfully, I can't imagine many women being able to cope as you have. Does that make sense?" She tilted her head.

"It does." I nodded. "I know this happened to me for a reason although I ask, why me some days?" I chuckled with confusion and shook my head. "My mom calls it being hard headed."

Ms. Clara chuckled. "Why not you, Olivia? I can't think of anyone better suited for this to happen to. That might sound hard, but God used you for his purpose and you learned some things about yourself in the process too. A lot of things!" Ms. Clara sat forward in her chair, moving closer to me to be more focused. "He could have been using you in Clyde's life also."

"Gosh, couldn't it have been someone else?" I was sarcastic.

"We didn't talk much about your previous relationships, but something tells me you were always the one in control and you were always the person leaving or giving the other person a way out. Sometimes the very thing we continue to run from will run after us until we face the thing inside ourselves we don't want to confront. And, God chose you to show you that. He's moving you forward and wants to prepare you." She spoke softly.

"Guilty again!" I smiled, trying to lighten up the conversation. "I did need to feel validated in my anguish and the judge gave me that. Is that wrong?"

"Not at all. We all need validation. It means we have a conscience." Ms. Clara smiled. "Why do you think you were always the one to break off relationships?" She changed the subject.

"I just didn't know what I liked and what I didn't and even what was acceptable in a relationship." I said dismissively, growing uncomfortable with the question.

"Why do you think that is?"

"I think it was because my parents' marriage was arranged and, although I witnessed a man's role and women's role, I did not really witness how two people related outside just day to day roles. It was all very confusing to me when I started dating."

"Interesting. Did you ever talk to your parents about dating?"

"Are you kidding? No. I feared being in trouble."

"Were you in trouble a lot as a child?"

"Actually, not hardly at all. I learned a lot from my older siblings what not to do and steered clear of it. We just didn't talk to our parents about dating."

"Was it hard dating as a young adult for you?"

"No, but I was confused. I was and still am very black and white and that doesn't bode well when you are dating. Dating is grey." I chuckled.

"Did you have a lot of dates?"

"Yes, actually."

"You strike me as someone that has very clear ideas of what you didn't want for sure, almost rigid," she said hesitantly. "Would you say you related well with your partner when you did date?"

"When I was younger, not at all, but I didn't know me. I think it has so much to do with your partner too, but I didn't say much because I didn't think it was my place."

"Meaning?"

"I never saw my mother question a thing, but yet she would be angry and resentful all day and I'd hear about it over and over. I still hear about it."

"Do you think she was trying to show you what not to do?"

"I'm sure there was an element to that, but the negativity didn't serve me well in my relationships." I laughed.

"So, why do you think you were usually the one to end relationships?"

"I haven't met anyone that fulfilled me."

Ms. Clara smiled. "Is there anyone you wish you didn't let get away now in hindsight?"

"No one," I said shaking my head sitting back comfortably.

"Do you think you approached Clyde with the same mindset?"

"I don't know what you mean?"

"You were curious and you dated him although you really didn't want to. You took the chance knowing you could break it off, if and when it didn't fulfill what you needed?"

"Yes. I get that."

"Do you think that was a good approach?"

"It worked for me before." I said shrugging my shoulders.

"Did it this time?"

"I had attitude then," I said dismissively.

"Yes, but you were and are older and we have to learn from our experiences. The stakes are higher now. Remember, Proverbs 4:23?"

"I'm sorry; I don't know what that says." I hesitated.

"*Above all else guard your heart, for everything you do flows from it.*" She paused. "That's simply just being careful. Don't let your heart grow cold or bitter, but do not give your heart to everyone either."

"I understand and I guess now I don't think you can just get in relationships with reckless abandon, thinking you can just break it off when you want either."

"I've asked you before, but I will ask again. Do you have any regrets or would you do anything different?"

"Probably not. I've learned over time, that every time something happened I learned from the experience and I wouldn't have that wisdom had it not happened.

"Good, and recognizing that is also a sign that you are growing from your experiences." She smiled. "So, what's left with court?"

"Just the attorney's fees."

She nodded. "They say time heals all wounds, but time also waits for no man. Sometimes we have to just give time, time. Does that make sense?"

"Yes. I know there's a time for everything; court took a long time, time couldn't come soon enough when I waited to go into labor and time is flying by with my little one who is already two years old."

"Exactly." She laughed. "And like the sands of the hourglass so are the days of one's life. There is indeed a time for everything!"

"And you know I also realize you can't buy time for anyone when they don't want to take time themselves."

"That's a good point, too! I'll have to remember that one." She glanced at her watch. "Not to sound cliché, but our time is up." We exchanged a laugh. "You have done well. I'm proud of you!" she said supportively. I felt better. I felt validated.

"Do you want to set up your next appointment for two weeks?"

"That works."

She smiled, bowing her head humbly.

I looked forward to the next time.

Fifteen
WISDOM

LIFE WAS GETTING BACK TO HOW it existed before all the court madness a few weeks ago. I surrendered to serenity knowing what I couldn't change and prayed for the courage to face everything else that needed changing. I had the greatest gift of life and I knew as much as I was blessed, much would be required of me to be and do all God called me to be. Jordan took me to newer depths in my heart and soul and gave me a renewed strength that I never could have imagined possible. I understood now, with much appreciation and humbleness, when people expressed to me their greatest accomplishment was their children, children who undoubtedly also bring the greatest joy!

Walter brought his youngest son over to hang out with Jordan for a play date. I observed Jordan interact and enjoy someone other than Mom to share his world and his toys with, and even relate with from a male perspective. Most times I was too close to appreciate and adore as an observer being awed by how much I loved this little being and how thankful and blessed I was to be his mom. I prayed Jordan knew he was loved before he was thought of, before he was born and for every day I am able to share with him.

As I watched Jordan play and interact, I witnessed his generous soul sharing toys, taking turns with a positive and inquisitive demeanor, quickly dismissing the thought that narcissism could be inherited; secure that nurture would indeed overrule nature.

My cell phone was ringing and as I hopped up from playing on the floor to look at the caller ID, I saw it was my attorney calling.

"Walter, do you mind, it's my attorney. I need to take this." I interrupted him as he played with the boys. He signaled with a head nod and shooed me away with his hands, as I walked toward the patio door, which also was the only area with a consistent signal.

"Hey, Ms. Debra." I opened the patio door and faced the tennis courts opposite my deck. There was a doubles match going on at the tennis court.

"Hey, lady. I'm receiving the order for the judge's response to our inquiries of the original order and your request for attorney's fees over my fax, as we speak. Do you want me to read it to you or shall I send it?"

"I have to read it sooner or later. Save me some time in my limited mommy time." Besides, it's Friday so I'll either have a great weekend or not so great, depending on what you tell me. It is what you tell me it is!"

"Okay, I'll be brief and hit the high points then. Don't interrupt me until I'm done," Debra instructed. "Looks like the child support addendum has been granted, so child support will go up and the judge denied his request to increase the travel expense credit and as we knew before, she ordered him to cover health insurance. I guess his attorney tried to argue or question the health insurance in their letter, so that's why the judge is reiterating it here." Debra took a deep breath. "Looks like the holiday changes were made as requested and she assigned the next three years summer visitation instead of arbitrary dates. The request for attorney's fees is coming over the fax now."

There was a long pause as I felt my nerves tingle and my muscles tense up.

"Granted! Guardian fees granted in your favor also."

"What?!" I said with unbelief. "Oh my gosh! Oh, thank God! ARE YOU SERIOUS?" I shouted. I was ecstatic as I began jumping up and down not realizing what I was doing until I looked over my shoulder and saw Jordan begin to start jumping also.

He began to squeal, "Mommy yump." He was giggling. I was 'yumping' for joy all right!

"Yes I am! As a heart attack! I told you and I couldn't be more serious! The judge had to stick to the law regarding visitation, but honesty and integrity always wins out. I knew you'd get the fees because of the way Clyde treated you through this entire ordeal and the things that he did were despicable!" Debra offered. "Not to mention he left a paper trail a mile long."

"I don't know how to thank you and I don't know what to say!" The thought crossed my mind to scream aloud, but I remembered the tennis match. I stepped back indoors as I saw the black sedan truck slowly coming up the drive and then turn in the direction of the other building. *Maybe the owner lived in the complex. Maybe I had been over reacting,* I thought.

"Don't say a word! Enjoy your weekend and we'll reconvene next week. Oh, and congrats! Good job on the attorney's fees letter. You did a nice job. You should write that book or at least be a legal writer."

"Thanks, Ms. Lady. I followed your lead with the samples you gave me, but for now I don't want to even hear the word legal." I was reminded how exhausting the ordeal had been or maybe I never forgot and it had become a way of life.

"You still need to think about writing that book though! Your story is so unbelievable and it needs to be heard." Debra sounded sincere.

"Maybe. We'll see. If I can ever find a way to stay up past nine." I chuckled. "Thank you, again!" I closed the patio door and hung up the phone. I resumed my jumping up and down with Jordan with plenty of smiles and giggles to go around.

I hoped God was smiling, too, knowing I was graciously thankful!

"I assume… good news?" Walter hesitantly asked. "Tell me, girl!" He nudged my shoulder.

"Awesome news! She increased the child support and get this... she ordered him to pay my attorney's fees *and* the Guardian's fees as I requested! I can't believe it! This is such a blessing!" I was ecstatic. I started jumping up and down, stopping to pick up Jordan and twirl him around. "God is good!"

Jordan let out a squeal. "HOORRAY!" *Yes,* I thought, *hooray indeed!*

Walter's son joined in.

"That's great! Any change on visitation?" Walter stood up and lifted me off the floor with a huge hug.

"No. We weren't trying to change visitation since the judge ruled on that after the trial. I'd have to open an appeal process to change that ruling." I sighed. "As much as I think Clyde is selfish and neglectful regarding Jordan's needs, I'm going to have to figure a way to manage the visits. I do believe Jordan is too young and shouldn't be away from his home and what is familiar to him and have his world turned upside down, or any child for that matter, because the parents aren't together and certainly not if one of the parents is unstable. At least, not until the child can talk. Children need to feel secure and have all the comforts they know. Stability and routine for a child this age is paramount, but apparently, the courts don't weigh those things in the 'best interest of the child'. I've read a lot of research that supports that and many states have moved to no overnights until age three; no questions asked, but unfortunately, many states still haven't." I was ranting.

Jordan was cruising alongside the ottoman table, as I noticed his eyes zero in on a tower of blocks within his reach that he'd previously stacked. In an instant, he stretched out his hand, knocking it down as he watched it crash to the ground. "Yowee!" He was delighted with his accomplishment, and plopped himself down to rebuild his fortress. I sat to join him feeling that no matter how many times I got knocked down, I would get back up again and keep rebuilding just like Jordan had done with the tower, time and time again, bigger and stronger each time. I wanted my son to learn, that as long as he kept trying, he could still stand and he could always rebuild when he falls down. *I am still standing.* Just like the Greenway.

"The judge did say she had to follow the law," Walter offered.

"I know, but why a child's emotional well being in one state is different than in another state is absolutely absurd to me. Ultimately, children become adults and the courts should govern with at least some uniformity at the state level where it starts, but don't get me started." I shook my head. "Maybe I should consider moving to a not so backwards state like Alaska. Children should be the interest of the Federal Government since they are eventually citizens in our society and our economy and especially since they are not entitled to rights as a minor. I guess all the other political mess and bureaucracy at the state level is why our children get overlooked." I was perplexed. "I just wish I could do something or join a coalition or advocacy group that fights for children's rights, but I know that's easier said than done. I can only imagine the number of women in the system that feel helpless and the even larger number that are worse off than me. Something has to be done! It's just unacceptable!" I was shaking my head. I was relieved to vent.

"You're probably not alone with your concerns. The system should feel the disparity they shoulder in their congested courts at the cost of innocent children especially considering the growing number and probably majority being raised in single parent homes these days," Walter said supportively. "Just keep doing what you are doing."

"Clyde's only got ten percent of Jordan's time, and that's if he takes his visits, so all he should hope for is a fun weekend with his son because that's about as far as anything he does with him will go. That's what I will focus on."

"Well, the parent that wants to visit when it's convenient shouldn't have much of a say in anything anyway!" Walter's tone grew short.

The kids continued to play, making all sorts of towers, sorting and lining things up, completely oblivious to anything outside their perfect world. Jordan busied himself, as he took a quick inventory of all his toys scattered about his playroom. I watched him deliberate which toy would be his next target to provide the most delight.

"You know the more I think on it, I didn't lose anything after all because I have Jordan and that's all that matters. Clyde thinks he's angering me, but I refuse to give him that satisfaction," I said. It was more of a proclamation and I was determined that wouldn't happen.

"Well, that's smart! He's just miserable, but he has to pay your fees now, so he's getting his."

"He'll never get anything because he's such a narcissist. This will only piss him off more and he'll try to get me back because he has to win. He'll spiral out of control sooner or later. This is about my son and only my son." I was getting aggravated spending another minute talking about this. I heard an engine idling outside and walked toward the patio to look out the blinds. I felt uneasy seeing the Black Escalade again.

"Knowing this guy's past behavior, he'll just go on being the victim. He's so self-serving that he'd be better off being gone, because there's nothing self serving about a being a parent," Walter said shaking his head. "And kids are smart! Everyone knows Jordan is who is because he's with you and it's all your doing!" Walter sensed my anxiety and walked over toward the window to look outside.

"I thought he would've been gone since he wanted nothing to do with me the first five months, but now he sees so much in Jordan that he's hanging on like a ticket to ride. Did I tell you about him wanting a trust fund with access in the event Jordan gets any money?" I said with as much disbelief as the look on my face. "I have an order that holds him accountable and it's enforceable and he should have learned by now, that I am not fooling around and will pursue the law for contempt and have him arrested just as quickly as he wants to violate it. This is my child and he'd better not try me!" I glanced at Jordan smiling and making faces of enjoyment and humming sounds of pleasure.

"While I'm not surprised with everything else you told me, it's still unbelievable that anyone could bring himself to ask the judge that, but there is no law for stupidity either. I still can't get over when you told me that he said he'd be nowhere around if you had a girl. You know, you're probably right and it almost makes me wonder that since the judge had to stick to the law regarding the visitation part, she ruled in your favor on the fees to make it a little uncomfortable for him because that piece was entirely up to her. It's just a matter of time for him."

"Yep, pretty sick and the sad thing is he hates me more than doing what is right and he comes across scorned, which is so unbecoming, but that's another story." The look of disgust crossed my face again. "He doesn't even call his son and he was the one that fought to get calls at the school to avoid interacting with me." I reached over to where Jordan was sitting and kissed him on his forehead.

"Of course, that's the narcissist needing to appear like the great dad calling his son to make himself look better and try to make you look like the bad guy, but I'm sure the school is on to him also," Walter said dismissively.

Jordan grabbed my leg and squealed.

"They are. He'll keep creating drama and wasting everyone's money and time or at least his own. Enough of that...it's Friday and my little guy is happy." I turned to pick up Jordan. Walter's son ran to grab his dad's legs.

"How 'bout some pizza, Jordan?" I looked at him with big googly eyes.

"Yeah! Mommy, pppizz-a." Jordan was in agreement.

Hawaiian barbeque pizza was calling our name.

Sixteen
FOUND

☞

"YOU LOOK GREAT! THAT DRESS LOOKS so comfortable," Ms. Clara said, admiringly smiling.

"Thank you." I sat down on the high-back chair next to the window. "It's good to see you!"

"It's been a few weeks since our last visit. How are you doing?"

"I feel good! I'm working on me and the things I can change."

"That sounds wise." She smiled. "You mean, instead of always thinking about what Clyde is going to do?" I sensed Ms. Clara's energy and tone was very relaxed. I felt it. Or, maybe it's the place I was in.

"That's exactly what I mean and it's refreshing not always having to be on the defensive. I'm not as exhausted. I feel good." My body exhaled with that declaration.

"Some people like drama because it gives them a sense of purpose."

"I don't see the purpose in that, but to each his own. No thank you!" Gesturing a stop with my hand.

"People without a purpose try to entangle others, manipulate and project drama to others, avoiding their own. It's almost a form of depression and addiction, which breeds the saying, 'misery loves company'." Ms. Clara nodded her head with affirmation. "So last time you were done with court and you were waiting on the fees. Have you heard?"

"Yes, and he has to pay mine," I exclaimed confidently. "I think this added fuel to his fire, but I will be ready to fight if I need to."

"That's a sad, but true statement!" Ms. Clara affirmed. She sat back in her chair as though comfort had set in. "You really do look great!"

"He's not fazing me and he's not stealing my joy of life, love and my amazing son."

"Love? Have you met someone?" Ms. Clara prodded, as she smiled raising an eyebrow.

"I'll just say, God does answer prayers." I smiled bashfully. "I actually met someone while I was in Chicago and we stayed in contact."

"Good for you. See, you needed to be in Chicago." Ms. Clara smiled approvingly as she nodded her head. "Do you like him?"

"I love him. I'm thankful," I said, thoughtfully thinking of Trevor.

"I'm so happy for you! You deserve it! I mean your life has been so clandestine," she said contemplatively.

I paused, a little confused. "Clandestine? Maybe I'm not sure I know what that means. What do you mean by that?" I questioned hesitantly.

"It means secret and I've thought about what you've been through and all the secrets you've faced. The courts failed to define the best interest of the child to protect themselves and remain impartial, your son's dad forged your signature and a death certificate and then you found out he was living a double life, from a private investigator, no less." She shook her head looking away. "I don't know what I would have done. Everything contradicted what you thought you knew and you had to uncover the truth. I'm sure you questioned life itself."

"I know I had angels watching over me and I had to stand strong for my child." I pressed my palms against my chest.

"If this were my child, I think I might have left the country," Ms. Clara admitted. "By the way, did you ever consider leaving?"

"Most definitely! How can a person not think of it with this madness? I thought about it often."

"How is Jordan doing?" She changed the subject. I heard the jingle of keys as my body relaxed back in the couch.

"Jordan is growing so fast and time is flying just like you said. I can tell when I look at him that he understands what is going on and I watch him process things and assess every angle of a situation before diving into it as if having reservation before calculating and deliberating his options."

"I wonder where he gets that." Ms. Clara chuckled.

"I recognize he has a special spirit like he taps into a higher meaning of things. I just want to be there for him to encourage, support and motivate him to be all he is called to be, while at the same time honoring that I am called to be his mom." I paused reflecting. "It's definitely our time and I can't think of a better time to enjoy this time. I just want to relish in all the blessings and all the joy of him." I felt empowered as I uncrossed my legs and sat up.

"Beautiful! You really have an amazing story!" Ms. Clara said, shaking her head and placing her chin in her hand, resting on her leg. "I really do think the courts need to step up and protect the best interest of the child in a way that is more reflective of our present day society and statistics of the time. There is strength in numbers and you can give others strength and encouragement. You should think about writing that book," she stated reflectively looking away.

"I'll give it some thought," I said casually. "I know I wouldn't want anyone to go through what I am going through." I contemplated. "I wouldn't even wish it upon my worst enemy."

"What I want to know is how you kept it all together? You've done great!"

"Ms. Clara, it was people like you and my attorney, friends and family, that never gave up on me for all the times I ranted and went on and on about everything in this process. Even before I got back to Charlotte there were random people from who knows where they came from supporting and offering help to me and giving me an unsuspecting encouraging word. They're all a part of my story and they were all there for a reason." Ms. Clara smiled, nodding approvingly. "I think knowing that my steps were ordered is what gave me the strength every day to do what needed to be done. Not to mention tons of prayer, yoga and meditation and growing some thick skin along the way."

"That's good advice to share, for sure. Not to mention the patience I know you had to have with the court system that so many people are caught in."

"That's another novel in itself. Don't start me on that one." I rolled my eyes. "I used to pray for patience, but now I know to be careful what you pray for!" I digressed. "Now, I'm learning to give time, time. A wise woman told me that." I smiled at Ms. Clara. I was thankful for her.

"I understand! Sometimes it's the crisis management that is more effective to teach patience then it is by definition, just like the *Serenity Prayer* says; accepting things you can't change, courage to change the things you can and the wisdom to know the difference," Ms. Clara offered.

"I agree! And realizing some people are just stuck on stupid also." I laughed. "I determined I'm the only person in control of my future and my happiness when I made the decision to be a mother and that meant standing strong with whatever came and not allowing others to keep me from my blessings." I exhaled, as I looked out the window overlooking the courtyard. It was peaceful and quiet.

"That has worked in your favor. Your child needs you to be healthy and strong, so you can care for and love him and oftentimes, it's the wisdom part that's important because you learn to choose which battles matter most. We have to make a new path for ourselves and true wisdom is in knowing which path to take. Would you say your faith allowed you to realize that?"

"It's been nothing but my faith!" I affirmed nodding my head.

"Let's talk a little bit about that. Did you always have faith before this happened?"

"I found my faith when I was twenty-one and really it started as a curiosity because all my friends went to church, but as life went on, it became a need for me. I found myself in situations needing strength from a Higher Power."

"Do you think you lost your faith along this journey?" Ms. Clara asked inquisitively, knowing where my healing needed to flourish. I followed.

"I think I was lost before this journey. I got the big head and assumed I was in control of my world, and I took my faith for granted. I still believed, but I didn't listen to the spirit inside me and I wasn't praying and being still. My faith became more of a habit than submission. I just thought I had it all and knew it all, but it wasn't until I found out I was pregnant with this guy that I realized I was lost and I was hurting." Ms. Clara listened closely. "That's when it occurred to me that God didn't leave me, I left Him and it was this journey that helped me find myself again!" I felt embarrassed, but I knew by asserting my errors I'd be stronger to confront my fears. "And all those people I met along the way that encouraged me were His messengers reminding me I wasn't alone. He never gave up on me." Warm tears began to stream down my cheeks. I wasn't ashamed.

"Sometimes that is how it happens and that's the way it's exactly supposed to happen. God used Clyde to bring you back to Him and He knew it had to be something pretty serious to get your attention." She spoke compassionately.

"Well, He got my attention. I feel so terrible that it took this to get me here."

"This place is your journey; a journey filled with love and hope with your son, and possibly your new friend also. If you didn't go there, you wouldn't be able to share your story either so don't feel terrible, feel triumphant for having being there." She paused. "And being here now."

"I guess I felt responsible for not making it different for my baby." I said sadly. "I have a most beautiful creation in life and Clyde tried to steal that from me inside out."

"But, he didn't. Your God is bigger! Do you believe it all happened to get you here because there is something bigger in store for you in your future?" she asked hopefully. "You know we go through things to prepare us for things to come."

"I do and through this all I did realize my steps have been carefully and masterfully ordered with each being cast from the last with a purpose toward my future. Some of my plans came together better than I could have planned and some I didn't even have to plan."

"That's the power of faith and you really didn't miss a thing. God is using you for His Glory and trust this man is not getting away with anything. He might think he is, but the bigger tragedy for him, is that he has lost so much already and when people fall into that hole, there is no getting out and then they just keep digging, instead of climbing and time waits for no man." Ms. Clara leaned over and placed her hand on my shoulder. "You on the other hand, have gained everything! Keep climbing!" she said proudly. "I remember a woman who walked in my office over a year ago that was lost because she doubted herself because she didn't trust her choices and decisions. That woman was just lost in herself, she just needed to come out, and it wasn't until her faith was tested was she able to withstand this seemingly insurmountable experience; facing single motherhood, moving and confronting someone else's deception and dysfunction and then a grueling court process from a system you felt betrayed you. Now, I see a very strong woman and a very beautiful woman who has so much to offer and so much to be thankful for! She's not lost anymore; she's found and the greatest part is she found herself!" Ms. Clara spoke powerfully. I was moved. I was crying.

"Thank you," I whispered, wiping my eyes. I nodded with affirmation. I felt joy. "I am found with a renewed spirit to live and to love and though I was bruised, I am not broken and I am healing. I did indeed stumble, but I am still standing. I am strong."

"Yes you are," she affirmed.

"I'm not focused on the setback anymore, but rather the most magnificent comeback in my life to give love and be love to Jordan. I've been taking interest in listening more and educating myself about people that exist in this world that don't always mean well by tapping into the wisdom to focus on what I can change while recognizing those things or people I can't and realizing there are no guarantees in life. I gathered the courage of just a mustard seed when I experienced the greatest gift of life to be born to me and it was in that moment that I knew I was favored to fight. I thank you for helping me do that."

Ms. Clara humbly dropped her head, nodding. "You did it! You found yourself!"

"I'm found," I declared. "I'm found! I AM found!" My voice grew louder.

"You've done great! And, I'm so proud of you. I'm always here and you can come and see me as often as you feel is appropriate or just whenever you want to talk and I'd love to meet that little one of yours. With a mom like you, he is destined for greatness!"

"Oh my gosh, an old lady that was watching her grandchildren at the track I sometimes ran at in Chicago said that to me one night."

"Another angel to help you stay your course. She was right," Ms. Clara said, raising her eyebrows. "So, can you tell me about this gentlemen you met in Chicago?" she teased. I heard keys rattle again.

"He's amazing." I smiled. "He's another one of God's angels to give me hope, so I wouldn't let go."

"I am so happy for you. Are you planning to marry?"

"What makes you ask that?" I was surprised and embarrassed. In a good way.

"I see it in your eyes that he's special." She paused. "And from what I know about you, that is no easy feat." We chuckled.

"He is special." I nodded, slowly. "Let's just say, if he asks me, I will be ready." I smiled.

"So, what are your plans?" She clasped her hands.

"He'll be moving here soon and we're going to take it one day at time." I smiled shyly.

"I meant for Olivia. What are her plans?"

"Oh. She's going to write that book!" I declared.

"Really?" Ms. Clara smiled deviously. "What made you decide?"

"As time went on in this process and I talked to people, I was amazed at the number of similar stories and single moms in similar situations, either going through something or been through something. I really do think, at least I hope, my story can help someone else or it will make someone take notice and change the system in favor of the best interest of the child. Things happen for a reason and maybe this happened to me to help make a change."

"It will! That's fantastic!" Ms. Clara put her hands over her mouth. "I want to buy the first copy and you have to sign it!"

"I won't let you buy it." I shook my head with a smile. "But I would like your permission to pen the sessions. Your services and these sessions were invaluable to my being; to not only validate my feelings in an effort to vent, but also to channel my anguish more powerfully with direction. I gained strength in our sessions and I was able to purge my soul of the negative energy while releasing the peace that was being discovered within. I have so much to be grateful to you for and I thank my lucky blessed stars for being able to rise above it all because of you.

I'm not crazy after all." I smiled amusingly. "You helped me to continuously find solace at every turn on my journey and I knew mine and Jordan's wellbeing would be ultimately unaffected. You helped me confront my emotions."

"I am so proud of you," Ms. Clara said, modestly looking away. She seemed choked up. "No, you are not crazy."

"I just want to say thank you! I'm happy and I'm sad," I said reluctantly.

"Why are you sad?"

"Well, because I've enjoyed our visits, but I don't know that I need to keep coming to visit with you anymore."

"You are found and I am here whenever you may want to talk to me. Job well done Olivia!"

"I found that light at the end of the tunnel like you said." I stood up slowly.

We said our good-byes until our paths crossed again, whenever that would be.

Ms. Clara indicated she was expecting another client as she reservedly followed me to the door. As I walked out the foyer doors, I fumbled through my purse for my keys shaking my purse for some sound of metal keys, but I heard nothing. Hurriedly, I took a deep breath and began to remove items from my purse. I noticed two missed calls from Walter on my phone. As I stood, I began retracing my steps recalling that I heard keys while in Ms. Clara's office and returned inside quickly, hoping not to interrupt her next client. The door was left ajar. With a slight knock, I opened it and stepped in.

"Hi, sorry, I think my keys may have…" I spoke fast, as I walked in to see Ms. Clara seated at her desk chair with the Kleenex box returned to her side, quietly crying. She sat motionless, staring at me. I stopped.

"Are you okay?" I asked gently.

"Olivia, I am fine." She paused, catching her composure "You are so brave and I am just so joyful for you and all you've come through. You've been through so much and I am just so glad I could help. You don't know it, but I had a similar situation before I met my husband and you helped me bring closure to that myself, for the first time. I don't know if I ever did because what you shared touched me at my core. Your story already helped one woman." She smiled through her tears, appearing somewhat uncomfortable, as she wiped her eyes. Her eyes were slightly reddened and her cheeks flustered. "I didn't stand strong and I didn't have that child."

"Thank you for working with me. I know I wasn't always easy." I wasn't sure what to say, but our souls comforted each other.

"No, thank YOU! You did great. You challenged me." She stood, holding out her arms for a hug. I was touched. This was the most emotion Ms. Clara had ever shown to me, maybe ever.

"Well, let me get out of your hair. I know you have another client." I walked to the couch and noticed the metal glistening in the crease of the cushion. "Just as I suspected." I grabbed my keys, dangling them in the air trying to lighten the air. "Thank you for you. For everything." I gave Ms. Clara another hug and felt her initial resistance melt away.

"Thank you, Olivia!" Ms. Clara whispered. "Thank you!"

⌒

As I settled in for the evening, I remembered I hadn't called Walter back, but decided I would in the morning and turned out the lights to get some sleep. I said my prayers, I was thankful for so much and for so many people. As Jordan slept, I gently picked him out of his bed and carried him to mine. There's nothing I wanted more than to snuggle next to the most important star in my world and have sweet dreams. I was found!

⌒

Dear Journal,

Some days when I look back when I first learned I was pregnant, I wouldn't have ever believed the next few years would have become what they did if someone told me, but I now realize everything happened for a reason. This is my story and I believe more than ever this is happening to me because my story needs to be told to help others stand.

I've learned over the past few years that I can only control what I can change and not people or things, but instead, only me and my reaction to those people and things. I've learned faith is a powerful thing and prayer is even more powerful and if I ever lose either of those; I've lost everything! I've learned I have to trust in the process even when I don't think one exists and that unless I believe in myself, faith and trust cannot thrive.

I wouldn't change a thing along my journey, not even moving to Chicago, because it took being lost to be found and it's that process that I am so thankful for. A process that afforded me wisdom; wisdom that brought the closure I needed to move forward and embrace my future.

I am most thankful for the blessing of Jordan to share love and happiness with my rainbow star. I am also thankful for Trevor and his armor and great family and friends that have been here for me. And, for Ms. Clara.

Faith, Trust and Believe!

With All That I Am,

Olivia

A large shadow moved against the side of the garage of the townhome, as Eli surveyed the area from his Escalade with his binoculars. His watch said ten-thirty. He remembered Olivia telling him there wouldn't be another visit for at least a month. He decided to dial.

Trevor picked up on the first ring when he saw Eli's name come across the caller ID. He had hired Eli to watch over Olivia during the court process.

"Hey, it's E. It's kind of late for a visit, but are you aware of a visitation this week at all? I'm trying to figure out if he's in town."

"No, not supposed to be one for three weeks. Why, where's Olivia?" Trevor asked anxiously.

"She turned her bedroom lights out five minutes ago, so she's in for the night, but I've been here fifteen minutes. I'm seeing a shadow against the outside wall and I think it's our guy."

"You've gotta go in there, E." Trevor spoke intensely.

"I do, but I need the bearings. I can't go in blind. Is Olivia's room upstairs or down?"

"Up."

"And where is Jordan's room?" Eli asked, shading his eyes from the glare of headlights that were coming up the lot to park close to him.

"Up."

"Okay, good. I can get to them before he does."

"Is there a patio on that first level?"

"Yes, on the back. Eli, you've got to get in there." Trevor's voice escalated. "I can't stand that I'm not there."

"Hold on. Wait a minute. Someone's driving up."

"Maybe it's just a tenant of another unit. E, you gotta get in." Trevor was impatient.

"Trevor, I know you love her, but you have got to remain calm. I need you calm."

Walter sat in his car, as he noticed a Black Escalade parked in the corner space. He had tried to call Olivia twice earlier, but didn't get a return phone call and decided to drive out to check it out himself since his boys were with their mom. He cracked the window and heard the engine still idling. The windows were dark and he couldn't make anything out. He debated his next move.

"Can you make anything out? Who's driving up?"

"From the overhead lamp post, I can see a silhouette of a masculine man inside."

Walter couldn't wait anymore, as he remembered the description of the car Olivia was concerned about as well as seeing it the other night. She hadn't called him back tonight, like they discussed and decided to confront and approach the vehicle. He opened his car door and quickly slammed it shut behind him. Walter wasn't afraid of much.

"Where is the shadow on the wall, Eli?"

"It's gone. Wait, the guy that just pulled up is walking towards my vehicle," Eli told Trevor, rolling down the window. "Hold on," Eli said. Walter's large frame was intimidating, but Eli quickly sized up that they were the same size and he had maybe a few inches on him.

"Excuse me, do you live here?" Walter asked in a confident, harsh voice. He noticed all the surveillance equipment on his dashboard, immediately growing suspicious.

"I don't, but I have a friend that lives here. I'm going to go in, but I was finishing up on a phone call. Do you live here?" Eli asked in a calm voice. He dropped the phone to his lap, turning on the speaker. He glanced at the wall of the townhome again, noticing some movement closer to the back end.

"I don't. I came to check on a friend," Walter said, getting angry. "What is your name?"

"I'm a private investigator. I'm checking on Olivia Thompson. Do you know her?"

"Is she in trouble? I came to check on her also. Have you been following her?" he asked nervously, following Eli's gaze in the direction of Olivia's unit.

"Your name?" Eli asked levelheaded, turning off the car.

"Walter Jones. I'm Olivia's friend and she didn't return my phone calls today and she's been checking in with me since her court mess started. Have you been following her?"

"Wait. Eli, he's cool," Trevor said over the speaker. "Olivia has talked about Walter."

"Who's that?" Walter asked, confused when he heard another voice.

"Trevor. I'm Olivia's—" Trevor's voice was loud over the speaker.

"I know who you are." Walter cut him off grudgingly. "Olivia talks about you all the time. She's a good girl. Don't hurt her because as soon as you mess up, I'm coming for her," he said sharply.

"Guys. This is beautiful, but Olivia is inside and I think our guy has decided to show up," Eli said, stepping out of the vehicle hurriedly, as he noticed the shadow completely move to the back of the unit. "T, gotta hit you back. I gotta get in there." He hung up, stuffing his phone in his back pocket.

"Walter, nice to meet you." Eli grinned, taking swift glancing strides toward the back of the property. Eli noticed the door was pried open and a metal stick was lying on the patio. Eli heard heavy breathing and Olivia's voice in distress. He couldn't make out what she was saying and jumped the railing of the patio. Walter was close behind. They saw Olivia's silhouette shadowed by a larger frame in the kitchen just as they heard glass crash to the floor.

"How dare you come into my house when I didn't invite you! This is my life!" I exclaimed, swinging the skillet across Clyde's head, knocking him down, falling to the floor. Walter rushed to catch me, as I heaved a sigh of air. "How dare you?" I said between breaths. I was sweating.

"It's okay." Walter caught me just before I collapsed. My body was limp.

"Olivia, are you hurt? Let me look at you?" Eli said, as he looked me up and down, stroking the hair away from my eyes.

"I came downstairs to get some water. I'm fine." I was disoriented. "Where's Jordan?" Eli searched the cupboards for a glass for some cold water.

Walter ran upstairs to Jordan's room to check on him, realizing I put him in my bed. He was resting peacefully. He ran back downstairs. "He's fast asleep."

"Do you two know each other?" I felt weak. "Eli what are you doing here?"

"We just met outside. I came to check on you because you didn't return my phone calls today. I got concerned," Walter said calmly.

"Oh, I'm so sorry! I was so tired! I just wanted to get some rest finally since court is over," I said, as sweat poured down my face and onto my silk t-shirt, now nearly soaked. "Eli, I thought you had a case?" I asked confused, looking up.

"I did. You. Trevor asked that I check on you while this court stuff was going on. He said you were really afraid the last time he was here. I'm sorry I didn't tell you, but he thought you would not allow him or me to help," Eli offered sympathetically, looking around as he walked toward the couch to grab a blanket and drape it across my wet body. "I also got a call from my Aunt Ernie and she told me to check in on you when I came to visit her. You have a lot of people who love you, Olivia." He smiled. "You have angels watching over you."

"Trevor is right, I would have been upset, but I'm just so thankful for all of you. I dreamt this would happen, but I thought I was going crazy." I began to cry. "Wait, Ernestine is your aunt?" Eli nodded. A shiver came over my body. I didn't believe in coincidences. I believed in God.

"She was sad when she told me her friend was moving to Chicago and then you moved back. When I was coming back and forth to see her, she told me to look you up. She didn't know I already knew you."

"And I was your case. It's a small world," I shook my head, looking at both of them. "And you drive an Escalade and you've been following me and that's how you knew I lived in a townhome?"

"Guilty." Eli dialed Trevor, knowing he'd be anxious for an update. "It was him. You're girl handled it. She's fine. Little shaken up. Jordan is sleeping," Eli explained to Trevor. "I don't think he's going anywhere soon." He glanced over at Clyde who was out cold across the floor. "I'll call the police."

"Can you put her on?" Trevor asked. Eli passed the phone to Olivia.

"Thank you, T. You are so kind, but you didn't have to do that or at least you should have told me." I was still softly crying.

"Sshhh! Baby girl, I got you." He spoke affectionately. "I am protecting my interest."

"You got me." I smiled. I felt safe hearing his voice. "You got me."

"Olivia, tell him thanks for me." Walter interrupted, almost forcing a smile.

"Get some rest. I'll be there in a few days," Trevor said, before ending the call. I hung up.

"Olivia, he's a great guy. Go to him. I'm okay." Walter surrendered somberly.

"Walter, you've always been there for me. I didn't know you still felt this way about me."

"I'll always care for you and I'll always be here for you, but that's a good guy and he really loves you. You deserve the best! I know I'm damn good, but he's best for you. It's a great story."

I rested my head on Walter's shoulder.

"I love you guys! I have angels."

Eli called the police and waited until they arrived. Walter offered to stay the night while I got some rest. I learned to let people help when they offered.

Jordan continued to sleep undisturbed through the night.

⁐

Dear Journal,

Thank You for allowing me to witness Your greatness and it is with humble gratitude that I feel blessed to be living. Time flies! It's been an amazing year of growth and I've learned so much about my faith. I have been made stronger in You and I am forever grateful for that!

I know You are using me in some way for Your glory even when I don't always know what that is, I pray You reveal that to me as I learn Your voice, Your spirit and Your ways in all the ways I go. To You I belong! I will always seek Your guidance and Your will and I pray I have the courage to do it!

Thank You for so many people in my life and I pray You continually bless them along their journey as You have blessed me on mine.

Help me to be the best mother I can be and to be strong for Jordan and for me. I'm still standing and I know You didn't bring me through my past to break me in the present or keep me from my future!

I have faith in my Creator, I trust in the process and I do believe in myself!

With All That I Am,
Olivia

∾

A few months later...

I was restless as I lay down to sleep, but decided to make the call.

The phone rang four times before the message service picked up. "You've reached Ms. Clara Bryant's office. If you feel this is an emergency, please call 911. If your matter can wait until regular office hours, please leave a message and our office will get back with you. Thank you and have a wonderful day."

"Hi. This is Olivia Thompson. I know the office is closed, but I was calling to schedule a visit with Ms. Clara. A lot has happened in just a few months, but I guess that's how life is. Just when we think we've gotten everything under control, something else happens and you find yourself upside down again." I giggled. "Well anyway, I have faith and I've come to appreciate your insight and would just love to talk to you!" I smiled thoughtfully. "Please call me back. Thanks." I hung up the phone and settled down to sleep.

I am strong, I said to myself as I closed my eyes.